W9-CQM-641

DATE DUE

AUG 0 5 2013

PRINTED IN U.S.A.

Gypsum, CO 81637
(970) 524-5080

Night Terrors

Night Terrors

Sean Rodman

orca soundings

ORCA BOOK PUBLISHERS

Copyright © 2013 Sean Rodman

All rights reserved. No part of this publication may be reproduced
or transmitted in any form or by any means, electronic or mechanical, including
photocopying, recording or by any information storage and retrieval system now
known or to be invented, without permission in writing from the publisher.

Library and Archives Canada Cataloguing in Publication

Rodman, Sean, 1972-
Night terrors / Sean Rodman.
(Orca soundings)

Issued also in electronic formats.
ISBN 978-1-4598-0420-3 (bound).--ISBN 978-1-4598-0419-7 (pbk.)

I. Title. II. Series: Orca soundings
PS8635.O355N55 2013   jC813'.6   C2012-907492-6

First published in the United States, 2013
Library of Congress Control Number: 2012952958

Summary: Dylan struggles with his memories of the death of his
younger brother while fighting for survival in a snowbound resort.

*Orca Book Publishers is dedicated to preserving the environment and has printed
this book on Forest Stewardship Council® certified paper.*

Orca Book Publishers gratefully acknowledges the support for its publishing
programs provided by the following agencies: the Government of Canada through
the Canada Book Fund and the Canada Council for the Arts,
and the Province of British Columbia through the BC Arts Council
and the Book Publishing Tax Credit.

Cover photography by Getty Images

ORCA BOOK PUBLISHERS
PO Box 5626, Stn. B
Victoria, BC Canada
V8R 6S4

ORCA BOOK PUBLISHERS
PO Box 468
Custer, WA USA
98240-0468

www.orcabook.com
Printed and bound in Canada.

16 15 14 13 • 4 3 2 1

For Mom

Chapter One

"Night terrors," says the psychiatrist. "A symptom of post-traumatic stress. Perfectly normal."

He smiles at me with polished teeth, gleaming white. Blond hair that's slicked back in perfect little lines, spotless expensive shirt, manicured hands. I'm slumped in a leather chair in jeans and a black T-shirt, feeling like the big wooden desk between us is more like a barrier between worlds. He's from a different planet. No way am I going to talk to this guy, no matter how much my parents want me to. The silence drags on.

"I can help you, but you need to open up," he says. That's why my parents brought me here—to get some help. Because they can't handle the screaming at night. Can't handle the way I've unplugged from everything, everyone, around me.

Like this plastic-faced shrink is going to help. There's no way I'm going to "open up" to this guy. Because if I tell him the truth, he'll think I'm crazy. The truth is, I sleep for four, maybe five, hours every night. And then the dream wakes me up. The dream is always the same, every time. It starts with me in my bed.

I open my eyes and see him standing there, watching me. Just a little shadow in the doorway. Six years old, small for his age. My little brother. I grunt out his name, wondering why he's woken me up.

"Sammy?"

He doesn't answer. Just watches me. I notice he's wearing his clothes, not pajamas. His Superman T-shirt is soaked through, and his hair is plastered down, wet. Then I smell damp leaves and the putrid scent of something rotting.

"Sammy—where the hell have you been? You know what time it is?" I whisper. He doesn't say a word but starts to shuffle toward me. And then I remember.

Sammy died months ago. I was in the river next to him when the current pulled him away. I tried to grab him, my hands scratching his slick wet back. Sammy was way out of reach downriver when he went down the first time. His head reappeared, looking back at me. Then he was gone under the black water, forever.

The worst part is, they never found his body. The search-and-rescue guys said it was probably pinned down at the bottom, under a log or something. I can't stop thinking about Sammy, lying down there at the bottom of the river, looking up at the daylight. Trapped.

So there is no way he survived. There is no way he can be here right now, sliding his feet across the floor, shadowy eyes fixed on mine. Sam stops at the edge of my bed, and his tiny hands reach up to me, scrabbling against my naked chest. Wanting me to pick him up. His hands feel like cold dead meat.

That's when I wake up screaming.

A week after the visit to the psychiatrist, the nightmares are worse than ever. My dad comes in and finds me in sweat-soaked sheets, my throat hoarse and sore. He sits close enough to me that I can smell the whiskey on his breath. The accident wasn't easy on him either. He listens as I mumble through tears, explaining the dream to him. When I finish, he takes his glasses off and just looks at me for a while.

"You remember when we saw that zombie movie last year?"

I nod, not sure where this is going. The film scared the crap out of me, although I tried not to show it to my dad.

"Right now, your mind is like a movie projector," he says. "It's throwing pictures on the wall. But they're just… images, ghosts. You're making yourself see scary stuff." He pulls up the sheets, smoothing them around me like I'm a little kid again. "You just need to turn the projector off. And the pictures…the ghosts…they'll go away."

He walks to the door. Looks back at me, one hand on the light switch.

"It's all in your mind," he says, "and ghosts can't hurt you."

He means well. But Dad is wrong. I don't find that out until a couple of months later.

Chapter Two

"For most of you, tomorrow means a final departure from Ravenslake Lodge and a return to real life. Which I know you are all absolutely devastated about," Edward says. A few people in the crowd laugh.

"However, as you may know, we recently dismissed two of our junior maintenance staff. So this year we need a few volunteers to help Harvey, our facility manager, close up the resort. It's an extra week of hard work, but at double pay. Please let Harvey know if you're interested." Edward turns slowly, scanning the crowd of hotel staff surrounding him. We're gathered in the main dining hall of the resort. The chairs and tables have been stored away already, so everyone is just standing around in groups. We've gathered into the tribes that keep the luxury resort running—the office staff, clean-cut and perky, even when they're off duty. Groundskeepers in overalls and ballcaps. The kitchen crew in their whites, piercings and tattoos peeking out from under the uniforms. And then there are the bellmen, like me—the guys who carry your bags, bring you room service. Like the others, I'm wearing a bright red jacket with my name embroidered on one corner in dorky lettering—*Dylan*. Not the most stylish but, like a lot of things at Ravenslake Lodge, you get used to it.

Edward has a thin face like an axe, and his narrow black eyes scan the crowd. "One final thought," he says. "I know that I have a reputation for…"

"Being a jerk." It's Tom, one of the other bellmen. He says it quietly, so only we can hear him. Wouldn't want to attract Edward's attention, even on the last day.

"…being a leader with exacting standards. I accept no laziness," Edward continues, shaking one hand for emphasis. When I started at the beginning of summer, I was told that with Edward, you screw up, you get fired. No second chance. I saw a few people go.

"I hope that, as you depart, you understand the reason for my standards. My insistence on self-discipline. My requirement for a true strength of character to work in a fine hotel such as this."

He smiles, thin lips forming a slash across his face. "It is my gift to you. Something you will carry away into the world, having been trained here at Ravenslake Lodge." He lifts both hands up, as if letting us all go. I see Tom roll his eyes at the dramatics. Edward winds up for his big finale.

"So as I thank you for your hard work, I think in fact you should be thanking me. For teaching you so well. For being a firm but fair leader. And to that I say, you are most welcome. It has been my honor." There's an awkward pause, then a ripple of polite applause as Edward walks away from the crowd.

The big dining hall fills with chatter. I see Tom heading out the door. I run to catch up. He grunts when I pull up to him, and we start walking down the gravel path toward the staff cabins.

"Dylan! D-Man! Edward was in good shape today, huh?" he says.

"Classic. I'm surprised he didn't fire someone right there, just to teach us all a lesson." He stops and leans toward me, lowering his voice. "Hey, I saved a six-pack from the party last night at the Point. You up for a victory beer while I pack my bag?" It's ten in the morning, but I'm not surprised. Most of the staff worked hard during their shifts and partied even harder off duty. Tom was always the ringleader, DJ and master of ceremonies for most of the late-night campfires and cabin parties. As long as we kept the action away from the resort grounds, out at a place called the Point, Edward didn't seem to notice.

"I'm good," I say. "It's a little early for me." Don't get me wrong— I've never complained about Tom or the parties. Far from it. They were the perfect prescription for my sickness, better than the drugs the shrink and my parents wanted me to take. I had spent the summer trying to blur out my old memories with a combination of sweat, beer and weed. The nightmares still came, but less often. Now it was all coming to an end. Ravenslake Lodge was closing up for the winter. The weather was already colder, and there was a chance of early snow. The last guests had already checked out, and soon a bus would come to drive us all back to the nearest town, two hours away. Then home. My stomach clenched at the thought.

"Your loss," Tom says. We walk up the creaky wooden steps to his cabin.

"What exactly is the victory you're celebrating?" I ask. Unlike the guest cabins at the resort, the staff cabins are basically shacks with eight beds and one bathroom, military style. Edward spares no expense when it comes to the guests. And goes totally budget when it comes to us.

"For surviving another summer up here. For surviving Edward." He looks at me like I'm stupid. He pulls out a beer from a little bar fridge at the end of the cabin, pops the tab with a hiss and flops down on the thin mattress.

"It wasn't that bad," I say.

"Seriously, D-Man? Stuck in the middle of a forest, hours away from civilization, working like a slave. Never mind all the stupid requests from guests who have more money than brains."

"So I guess you're not staying on?" I push aside some laundry piled on the bunk across from Tom and sit down.

"'Course not," he snorts. He squints and puts on a pirate voice. "A city is waiting to be plundered. Ladies to be deflowered. Gold to be…whatever." He takes a swig, then stares at me. "Wait—you're thinking about closing up the lodge?"

I shrug.

"No, no, no." Tom pushes himself back upright. "You're young—you need to fly free. Go home. You want to be up here with just Harvey and Edward? Stuck in the woods for another week?"

"I don't know. I wasn't planning on it. But I could use the money." The reality is, I have no plan for after I leave this place.

"It's not worth it and you know it. You think Edward is bad when he has fifty staff to torture? Think about what it'll be like with just you in the crosshairs. You know he used to be head chef of the kitchen before he was promoted to manager? Ran the kitchen like it was the army. Drills and everything. *Ca-razy* stuff. Apparently, the owners told him to tone it down when he became manager. But you've seen what he's like."

Yeah, I have seen Edward in full military-sergeant mode, screaming at a server until she cried. So far my strategy has just been to do the job and stay out of his way. But Tom is right—I won't be able to hide from Edward now.

Tom leans back on his bed. He smiles like he's been saving the best for last. "If that's not bad enough, it's nasty up here when everybody leaves. Bears move back in. Weather turns cold fast. It could even kill you," he says in a dramatic voice.

"You're full of it," I say, chucking a sock at Tom.

"No, seriously," he says. He drops his voice, even though there's no one else in the cabin. "Last year, I hear that they were closing up and a kid went missing. Never found him. They hushed it up—not good PR for a five-star resort. But I figure he was eaten by a wolf." He leans in. "Or a sasquatch." He cackles at my expression, finishing off his beer. I laugh too.

"At least you won't be here," I say. "I'll think about it, all right? Thanks for the warning."

The truth is, it's not that I want to stay. Or care about the money. It's that I don't want to go home. Before I left, everything at home reminded me of Sammy. Didn't help that my dad was drinking more, always picking fights with my mom over tiny little things that didn't matter. My friends were no help. They talked constantly about graduation outfits, whose party was the best, who got laid last night. The most important stuff in the world to your average eighteen-year-old. Stuff I just didn't care about anymore. In fact, I didn't care about anything or anyone. And the nightmares kept coming back. Almost every night.

So I ran away, hoping I could leave all my problems behind.

That's not quite true. I'm too responsible—or too lame—to just take off and hit the road. I did the next best thing.

After I graduated last June, I found a job in the middle of nowhere. Ravenslake Lodge. A big rambling hotel in the center of a national park, built way back in the 1930s. My parents thought it would be healthy for me to take a year off before I went to university. Get a change of scene. Although I think they really just wanted me out of sight, where I wouldn't remind them of Sammy.

I give Tom a final fist bump, and he gives me the rest of his six-pack as a going-away present. I crunch along the gravel path past the other cabins, past a cluster of hotel staff walking down to the parking lot to meet the bus. I find Harvey at the maintenance shed, fixing a broken screen door laid out on a pair of sawhorses. He turns and lays down a pair of wire clippers. He pulls off his work gloves to shake my hand.

"Dylan. You come to say goodbye?" he says, his deep voice booming through the shed.

"Nope," I say. "I want to stay on."

Chapter Three

The bus leaves a cloud of diesel behind in the gravel parking lot as it pulls away. I see Tom waving from the back window—a big smile, and then he gives me the middle finger. Class act, that guy. The bus is almost around the corner when Harvey puts a big hand on my shoulder.

"Let's get your stuff moved into the Swamp," he says.

"Swamp?" I ask. We start to walk back up the hill.

"Yeah. It's old and a little run down. You'll stay there while we close up everything else. I'm sure you can tough it out for a week."

We walk past the staff cabins and down a little trail, away from the main part of the resort. The resort is laid out like a bunch of half circles, with Raven's Lake running along the one edge. The main hall, with the kitchen, dining room and offices, is the inner point of the circle. Then there's a half ring of guest cabins. Small houses, really, with all the luxuries. Finally, a half ring of staff cabins, the maintenance shed, the generator. All the stuff that keeps the place running but the guests don't want to see. And then, outside of all those semicircles, the Swamp. It's tiny, way smaller than the regular cabins, and it looks like it must be fifty years old. Hopefully, the roof doesn't leak.

Harvey goes to unlock the door to the Swamp, but it's already open. We walk into the small space. This is going to be like living in a garden shed. There are two beds, one on each side. The wall above one mattress is covered with pieces of paper, mostly pencil sketches of superheroes. A guy with long dark hair in a ponytail is pinning another drawing to the wall. He turns, stares at me and Harvey. He looks a little like John Lennon, with his long hair and round glasses. Doesn't say anything. I recognize him—Josh, a dishwasher. Tom called him "Silent J." No surprise, then, that Josh mostly kept to himself.

"Hey," I say, taken aback. "I thought it was just me helping out." Josh looks awkward. Harvey speaks up.

"Naw, Josh volunteered as well," says Harvey. "Figured I could use two pairs of hands." He studies me, then asks, "You're all right with sharing the cabin, right?"

"Yeah," I say. "Yeah, whatever. It's fine. I just didn't know." I throw my duffel onto the other bed, and Josh turns back to his drawings.

"Good. You two meet me in Edward's office in ten minutes. We'll go over the work." Harvey clomps down the front stairs. I unpack my bag in silence, not sure what to say to Josh. He finishes sticking pictures on the wall, then pulls out a sketchbook and starts drawing. This could be a long week with Silent J, I think. Maybe I shouldn't have stayed. Maybe should have found another way to avoid going home. As if he's reading my mind, Josh suddenly speaks.

"Go," he says quietly.

"What?"

"We need to go," he says. "It's been ten minutes."

"Oh, right," I say. "Thanks. I lost track. Yeah, we better go check in at the office."

We leave the Swamp and walk over to Edward's office in the main building, dry leaves swirling across the paths.

"Those drawings," I say. "Are they all yours?"

"Sort of. I mean, they're all copies of Golden Age heroes, not original ideas or anything. But basically I'm copying Stan Lee and Steve Ditko." It's the longest I've ever heard him speak, but it might as well be another language. He sees my confusion and mumbles, "Yeah, the drawings are mine."

"You're pretty good," I say. "You could sell them."

"I don't think so," Josh says. "They're just for fun. But thanks."

We come around the back of the main building. Wooden timbers frame the staff entrance, an old, ornate double door inlaid with carvings of moose, beavers and bears. Inside, the carpeted hallway has more wilderness stuff on the walls—a couple of oil paintings of forests, the head of a deer with massive antlers. The doors to the offices are all closed and locked except for Edward's, which is half open. We pause at his door, unsure if we should enter.

"You're late," comes Edward's voice from inside. "Please note that this will be the last time that you are late for me." I push open the door, and we see Harvey in his big brown overalls, filling a chair across from Edward's desk. We walk in and stand awkwardly in front of them. Edward's office is pretty sparse. A few books on a shelf behind his big oak desk. There's a worn bundle of cloth on the shelf as well. I recognize it as a knife roll, the kind chefs use to store their best knives. On the wall are some certificates and a few awards for cooking.

"Go easy on them," says Harvey. "They were just getting settled." Edward glares at Harvey, then stands behind the desk.

"Harvey, easy is not a word that is appropriate here," he says. "Protecting this hotel against six months of winter is not an easy task. I expect all of you to work to your utmost. These will be long days, and there is much to do as the weather worsens. Harvey, what is the first order of business?"

Harvey checks a clipboard with a long list on it. He quickly describes a bunch of tasks. Installing storm shutters on all the cabin windows. Storing the floating docks in the boathouse. Painting. Sanding.

"That's a lot to do in one week," says Josh.

"Yeah," Harvey agrees. "We're gonna need to give'er. I'll head down to the maintenance shed now and get the supplies ready for you. We've still got a couple hours of daylight today. We'll get a good start on it." He slaps me on the shoulder as he walks past. I turn to follow him, but Edward stops me.

"Wait," says Edward. "Both of you. I want to clarify something."

He walks slowly around his desk until he is in front of Josh, then stops. His eyes flit between Josh and me. Distantly, I hear the muffled thump of the heavy wooden door closing as Harvey leaves the building.

"Josh, look at me," Edward says. Josh lifts his eyes from the carpet to meet Edward's glare, then looks away.

"I said, look at me," Edward repeats firmly. "As far as I can tell, for the entire summer you were a shadow on the wall of this hotel. What did you do for us?"

"I washed dishes," mumbles Josh.

"That's right. You washed pots and pans. A monkey could do that job, Josh. So I'm quite unclear why Harvey allowed you to volunteer."

"He worked as hard as anyone else," I say. If anything, all Josh seemed to do was work. He never partied with the rest of the crew.

"I didn't ask you, Dylan. But let's find out if you are correct. Let us have some proof that Josh is worthy of working here. We'll accomplish one special task before you go and see Harvey."

Chapter Four

Edward leads us down to the resort dock and right to the end of the pier. The lake is flat and gray, a reflection of the clouds above. On the other side of the lake, some of the trees still have red and orange leaves on them, forming a bloody slash on the horizon. Small waves ripple across the surface of the lake as a cold wind blows across it. I've avoided coming down here all summer. Being close to the lake makes me nervous and tense, even though I know it's not the same as the river in my dream.

"There," says Edward, pointing at the raft. It's a wooden platform, floating about a hundred and fifty feet offshore. "Swim out to the raft and untie it. I'll bring the boat around, and we will pull it to shore." Josh looks at the dark water. He doesn't say anything.

"Why not just drive out together?" I say, and I point to the hotel boat, a little inflatable rubbing gently against the pier. "The water's pretty cold."

Edward spins to face me.

"Did I ask for your opinion? I said that I wanted proof. That Josh is willing to work hard. He needs to learn to do what it takes," he says. "Perhaps you would care to join him in the water?" I look away from Edward and out across the lake. My stomach clenches. I shake my head.

"It's okay, Dylan. I'll go get my swimsuit," says Josh. He starts to walk back toward the Swamp, but Edward puts a hand on his chest.

"No time. You heard Harvey. We have a great deal to do," says Edward.

"In my clothes?" Josh looks to me, then back to Edward. He looks scared, confused. We both know that Edward has a reputation for being mean. For humiliating staff like this. But nobody objects because they don't want to lose their job. Same with me. I don't want to make myself a target. So I shut up.

"Quickly," repeats Edward, his voice a little louder. "Now, Josh. Do as I say."

Josh flinches, then pulls off his sweatshirt. He carefully takes off his glasses and puts them on top of the sweatshirt. Then he kicks off his shoes and, leaving his jeans on, clumsily leaps into the water. I hear him gasp as the cold water closes around him.

For a moment, he hangs on to the side of the dock. He looks at me, blinking nearsightedly. I think about just reaching down and pulling him back up. Ending this. But then he starts to swim out to the raft.

A minute later, I can tell he's in trouble. He's obviously not a strong swimmer to begin with. The weight of his jeans, the temperature of the water—they're both dragging him down. He's maybe a third of the way to the raft when he goes under.

I wait for him to come back up. He'll come back up. Josh said he could do this. He wouldn't get in the water if he didn't think he could do this. My heart is slamming in my chest. Josh's dark hair rises up and breaks the surface of the water. I can see him gasping, thrashing. He turns to look back at the dock. At us.

And I swear, for a moment, I see Sammy in the water. Not Josh.

I blink and he's gone again. There are only waves where he was a second ago.

I can't let this happen again. But I can't move my feet. I'm frozen in place, unsure. Terrified of getting in that cold, dark water.

I turn to Edward, shouting, "Go get him! Get the boat! Don't you see? He's in trouble!"

"In a moment," says Edward quietly, staring steadily out at the lake. "This is a test of character." I realize that he's enjoying this. He's got a weird look in his eyes, like he's hungry. Like he can't wait to see what happens. And I suddenly know that Edward wants to see Josh hurt. I don't get why—I don't get what sick game he's playing. But if I don't make a move, Josh might not make it.

It's up to me.

Chapter Five

It's as if that realization unlocks me. Unfreezes me. I rip off my sweat-shirt and hit the water, massive strokes chewing up the water as I churn toward the raft. The water is so cold that it hurts to breathe. But I don't stop. When I get to where I last saw Josh, I dive down. Everything goes silent and black. Except there's a part of my brain yammering away, telling me I'm going to die. Telling me that I let Sammy die. That I'm going to screw up again. But I keep diving, hands flailing in the darkness, reaching out.

Nothing.

My lungs burn. I start to slow down, kicks getting weaker. I can't do it. One more stroke with my arms, and that's it. I can't resist as my body is pulled back toward the surface.

My fingers brush against something warm. Josh's hand. I grab it, then his arm. Kick hard. A few seconds later, we both break the water, gasping, coughing. Josh's eyes flicker open, but he's too weak to swim. One arm across his chest, I slowly pull Josh back to the dock. Edward is still standing exactly where I left him. He doesn't make a move to help as we haul ourselves onto the dock. We lie there, exhausted, just trying to breathe. Starting to shiver from the cold lake breeze.

"That was dramatic, Dylan," says Edward, "but unnecessary. I'm sure Josh would have found his way back to the pier." He starts to walk away from us, then turns back. "Remember to report to Harvey once you've dried off."

Josh and I can't speak. And I wouldn't even know what to say. Finally, the cold wind starts to bite. We pull on our sweatshirts and leave the docks for the cabin. As we walk past the boat bobbing gently against the dock, I look down and stumble a little.

"What?" Josh asks.

"Nothing," I say. I don't want to freak him out more, so I just keep walking. I don't tell him that there wasn't even a gas tank in the boat.

I don't think Edward ever planned to go and get him from the water.

Chapter Six

I don't see Josh for the rest of the day. Harvey doesn't know what happened, I guess, and I don't know how to tell him. Don't know if I should say anything. So Harvey just splits us up, and we go to work. I spend the after-noon hammering storm shutters onto guest-cabin windows. Three nails across the frame at the top, three at the bottom.

Seven windows per cabin. I try just to focus on the job, lose myself in the repetitive action of hammering. But sometimes, when I close my eyes, it's like there's a bunch of snapshots waiting for me.

The bump of Josh's head above the dark water, just as he goes under.

Edward staring out at Josh. Perfectly still, waiting. No, not just waiting— anticipating. Enjoying the struggle.

The pale glow of Josh's skin through the murky water as I try to pull him up. Just like Sammy looked.

I smash the hammer down, again and again, pounding nails into the frames of the windows. The sound rings out across the empty hotel grounds and into the forest.

Around midafternoon, Josh's voice crackles through my walkie-talkie, asking me to meet him in guest cabin three, Pineview. He sounds excited, so I jog down the looping path to meet up with him. When I get there, he's out on the porch, kneeling in front of a metal box. It's one of the live traps we use. In the middle of a park, you end up with a lot of wildlife coming through. We set up these traps inside the attics of the cabins to keep the squirrels from nesting up there. But there's something bigger than a squirrel banging around inside this one.

"Check it out!" says Josh. "He's pretty pissed." I kneel down beside him and peer into the box. Two dark eyes surrounded by a mask of black look back at me. The raccoon hisses, and Josh and I both flinch.

"Whoa. How'd he squeeze into the trap?" I ask.

"I don't care how he got in there. How are we going to get him out?" says Josh. He's got a point. With squirrels, we throw the trap in the back of the pickup, drive down the road, then pop open the trap and watch them scamper away. Probably right back to the cabins, but whatever. A big, angry raccoon is a little different though. I don't want to be the one to open the door of the trap, that's for sure. I'd be liable to lose a finger. Or get rabies.

"Harvey'll know what to do. I think he said he was going to be in the office. Grab one end." Together, we gingerly carry the long steel box down the path toward the main building. The raccoon doesn't appreciate the ride—there's a lot of hissing and thrashing around. But we get to the rear entrance without any damage to him or us. We leave the box outside while we search for Harvey. No sign of him. Until we walk by the closed door to Edward's office.

"Are they arguing?" whispers Josh.

"...standards. You need to be decent to them," Harvey is saying. I can't make out all the words through the heavy door.

"Standards are exactly the problem, Harvey. They need to meet my standards, or they go. I have always been very clear about this."

"That's one thing," Harvey says. "But you're starting to go beyond the line. You know that." Edward says something, but it's too muffled for us to make out. Josh motions for us to go, but I shake my head and knock on the door. The voices halt, then Edward opens the door. I can see Harvey slumped in the chair across from Edward's desk, just like the last time we were here. He looks tired, worried.

"Can I help you?" says Edward. He stares impatiently at me as I start to explain about the raccoon. Then his expression changes a little. He interrupts me.

"Where is it?"

"Outside," I say. "We didn't know where to take it."

"Fine. Leave it there. I'll take care of it later."

"You will?" says Harvey from his chair. Edward turns to face him.

"Yes, Harvey. I do have some skills beyond management, you know. You all have enough work to do. I'll take care of it later." I see Harvey's eyebrows lift, but he doesn't argue.

"Back to work, boys," says Edward. He closes the door while we're still standing there. Josh looks at me and shrugs. As we walk away from the main hall, I can faintly hear the raccoon rattling his steel cage. The sound of something trying to escape a trap. For some reason, the sound stays with me as I pick up my tools and get back to installing the storm shutters on the windows.

The sun sets early at this time of year. By five o'clock, the woods around the cabins have become nothing but shadows. Too dark to work. I pack up my tools and head for the Swamp, stomach grumbling. We're responsible for making our own meals with a stock of supplies and a little campstove in the cabin. The main kitchen is locked up, shut down and off-limits. Or so I thought.

"Dylan, meet me at the kitchen loading dock," Josh's voice crackles through the walkie-talkie. Not sure what's going on, I walk around the back of the main hall and stand outside the big metal rolling door of the loading dock. No sign of Josh. Then the door clatters up just enough for Josh to peek out. He smiles and motions for me to slip through.

It's pitch-black inside, but Josh has set up a couple of flashlights for light. The huge space gleams with long polished stainless-steel counters and big copper pots hanging on the walls.

At this time of day, when there are guests, the kitchen is filled with a dozen cooks. Now there's just Josh, standing over two pans on the gas stove.

"How'd you get in here?" I ask.

"You work in the kitchen all summer, keys go missing. Sometimes I found them. And didn't return them."

"Nice. Won't Edward figure out we're in here though?"

"No. Keep the lights off, the noise down. Clean up afterward. He'll never figure it out."

I shrug. "That smells awesome. What are you making?"

"Just some pasta. I made enough for both of us. Hope that's okay." My stomach grumbles. Yeah, it's more than okay. I was planning on cooking up my specialty—a peanut-butter-and-jam sandwich. The mountain of spaghetti and fragrant sauce Josh serves up is way, way better. We eat at one of the counters on a couple of stools. After I've cleaned my plate, I let out a satisfied belch.

"Where'd you learn to cook like that?" I ask.

"I just watched the cooks in here. Couldn't spend all my time focusing on scrubbing pots. I'd go crazy."

"Maybe I was wrong about the artist thing—you should definitely be a chef."

Josh smiles and shakes his head. Then I have a great idea for how to finish off the meal.

"Hey," I say, "you want a beer?"

Chapter Seven

I snag the rest of the six-pack that Tom left for me from its hiding place under my bed. Then we head down to the Point. When the staff wanted to party and get away from it all, this was the place. Back up the main road, then down a deer trail to the clearing. We use our headlamps to light our way, our breath making little clouds in the cooling air. By the time we get to the clearing, the moon has risen. It throws a white glow on the trees around us. Josh and I work together to build a fire in the pit. Pretty soon we're slumped in a couple of broken-down chairs that Tom rescued from the maintenance shed. Beer in hand.

We don't say much at first. Just watch the fire and check out the stars. Then there's a flicker across the sky, and a wave of light. Then another. The aurora borealis, the northern lights, are coming out. I never saw them before I came up here—huge curtains of blue and white light that ripple across the sky.

"Better than TV," I say.

Josh laughs. "I dunno. I'd be up for some channel surfing right now. I miss my cable."

"So why did you stay up here?" I ask. "Edward clearly has a hate-on for you."

"Yeah," Josh says. He takes a big slug from his can. "I guess I thought he wouldn't be so bad. I mean, I stayed under the radar during the season, watched him tear up other people. He fired, like, ten guys in the kitchen. I just kept my head down. Now he's getting worse though."

"So leave. Just walk away."

"Naw. Then I'd have to go home. That's worse." Josh drains his beer, then crumples the can and drops it to the ground. Maybe Josh and I have more in common than I thought.

"What do you mean?" I stare at him, watching the firelight reflect in his round glasses.

"I don't want to talk about it. Trust me—whatever Edward throws at me, it's not worse than what I've put up with already."

"I'm not sure about that. Out on the dock, I think he was enjoying watching you go under."

Josh looks at me a little uncertainly. "I saw him do this sort of stuff with other guys," he says. "Like he said, he likes to test people."

"I'm just saying, maybe you need to stand up to him a little more. You need—"

"Dylan, you think you got this all figured out?" Josh snaps, cutting me off. "You don't get it. I'm used to it, all right? My dad pulled shit like this on me all the time." He yanks up one sleeve of his jacket, showing me his arm. There are little white dots—scars. "Cigarette burns. I get Edward, okay? You fight back, it gets worse. So you just...deal with it and move on."

I just stare at his arm.

"You get it now? It's nothing new. Nothing I can't handle. So just shut up and toss me another beer," says Josh. I reach down beside me, and my fingers close on the cool metal skin of the can. Then I freeze.

Someone is watching us.

At first, I think it's a weird shadow being thrown from the northern lights, or the fire. But it's not. I slowly stand up, my eyes fixed on the figure standing in the shadows just on the edge of the clearing.

"Who's that?" I ask quietly.

"What? Who?" Josh stands up too and tries to follow my gaze. "I don't see anything."

But I can see him clearly. My height. Red jacket like mine.

"Is it Edward or Harvey?" says Josh. "It's got to be one of them. We're the only ones up here."

That's it. Edward. Of course. He probably followed us to the Point, looking to bust us. Creepy psycho. I stand up.

"Hey!" I shout. Maybe it's the solid buzz I have from the beer, or maybe I'm still reacting to what Josh just told me, but suddenly I'm mad as hell.

"Yo, Edward. Get over here!" I start walking away from the circle of fire-light and toward the woods. The dark shadow stands there. Staring. Probably laughing at me. "Yeah, you! I'm talking to you!" My voice sounds crazy loud against the stillness of the forest night. I whip my half-empty beer can at him. The guy doesn't move a muscle. I start running toward him.

And then I'm standing right where he was. And he's gone.

Josh catches up to me. His breath makes clouds in the cold night air.

"How'd he do that?" I say. I fumble my headlamp from my pocket and click it on. The leaves and dirt are covered in a thin layer of frost. No tracks. No sign that anyone was there.

"You sure you saw someone?" asks Josh.

"I don't know," I say. "I don't know what I saw."

Chapter Eight

Maybe I should be grateful. It's a new nightmare this time.

Not the old one with Sammy stumbling toward me in the dark. This time, I'm the one who is underwater. My feet are stuck down in the cold mud and weeds. I'm staring up, watching oily sunlight play across the surface. My chest is empty, and I know I'm going to drown soon.

But I'm not panicked. Instead, a kind of weird calm settles over me. Then I hear a hollow knocking sound echo through the water. I look around, trying to find the source of it. Nothing but murky blackness. The banging gets louder. I see someone, just on the edge of my vision. Someone like me, down here on the bottom. In a red jacket. Sammy? No. Maybe—Josh? Again, I don't think so. I suddenly gasp, lungs filling with cold water. The figure in the red jacket holds out his arms, trying to give me something. It's small, brown. A book, maybe? The knocking sound gets louder, coming from all around me.

I can't see. I can't breathe.

Noise slams me awake. Someone is banging and yelling on the door of the Swamp. I throw off my blankets and yank on some jeans. Josh is fumbling to put his glasses on, still tangled in his sheets. When I open the door,

I see Harvey and Edward standing there. Both of them look pissed.

"Get your clothes on," growls Harvey. "Follow me." I don't think I've ever seen Harvey look angry like this before. Edward just looks smug. Josh and I pull ourselves together and head outside. We walk behind Harvey, his footsteps visible in the thin frost on the ground. The sun isn't up over the trees yet—how early is it?

We stop in front of one of the staff cabins, number seven. It's already sealed up for the winter with big plywood sheets over the windows. Harvey leads us inside and turns on the light. The place has been trashed. Beds are tipped over, sheets ripped up. In one spot, there are big gouges as if someone has jammed a knife into the wall again and again.

"What happened?" I ask Harvey. But Edward answers.

"Don't pretend to be innocent," he says. "We know about your party last night."

"What?" I look at Josh. He's as confused as I am. "What are you talking about?"

Edward steps forward and holds up a crumpled beer can. From last night. The one I threw at the figure in the shadows.

"You were watching us," I say flatly.

"Watching you? No, I found this can, and another, out at the Point on my morning walk. It's my habit to keep an eye on the Point. Such reckless behavior can happen out there."

"So we had a couple of beers," says Josh. "We had nothing to do with... this." He gestures at the wreckage. Edward's face twists into a grimace.

"Don't you dare lie to me!" he barks. He steps toward Josh, and for a second I think he's going to slap him or something. But Harvey quickly puts himself in between the two.

"Edward," he says. "Give us a second, all right? I'll take care of this from here on in." Edward stares at Harvey, breathing hard. Then he spins around and slams out the screen door. Harvey watches him leave, then turns to us.

"Look," says Harvey, "I know something went on between Edward and you guys yesterday. The guy's got a mean streak. Right now, it's worse than usual. I get that. But is this your idea of revenge or something?" He looks from Josh to me, his brow furrowed. "You guys are better than that."

"We didn't—" I begin.

"I don't want hear it. Just get to work. Fix this."

Two hours later, we're just finishing cleaning up the cabin. And still trying to figure out how this happened.

"Maybe it was another raccoon?" suggests Josh as he sweeps up some shards of glass near the back of the cabin.

"I don't know. There's no food or anything in here. Windows are still sealed up. The door wasn't broken." I examine the big marks on the wall. They're only in one area, deep scratches where a wooden plank of the wall meets the linoleum floor. "And this doesn't look like claws."

"But that doesn't make sense. It's not you. Not me. Not Harvey," says Josh. He stuffs more ripped-up sheets into a big green garbage bag.

"Edward?" I say. I feel the gouges in the wood. What the hell made these marks? The plank is popped out a little from the rest of the wall, almost like it's been pulled loose. Harvey will make us replace that. More work.

"No," says Josh. "He's mean, but he's not crazy."

Chapter Nine

For the rest of the day, Harvey works Josh and I pretty hard. He's not his usual self—he keeps checking up on us. Grumbling that we aren't moving fast enough. I want to try and explain to him that we didn't cause the damage. Or talk to him about Edward. But I know it will just sound like excuses. And Harvey isn't big on excuses. So instead I just put my back into the work.

By the time we finish, we're so wiped that we barely make it through dinner. An hour after that, Josh is snoring away in his bed. I lie there for a long while, staring at the ceiling in the dark. If Tom were here, I'd steal a couple beers from his stash and get to sleep that way. Eventually I give up trying and prop myself up on my bed. I pull out my cell phone, and its green glow dimly illuminates the cabin. There's no reception up here in the middle of the park. But I can still play games on it. Use Tetris to keep the nightmares away. I think I have the sound turned off until the phone bleeps. Josh snorts, then rolls over to squint at me.

"What time is it, Dylan?" he says, fumbling for his glasses.

"I don't know. Maybe two?" I answer. "Sorry."

Josh sits up and pulls his hair back into a ponytail. He doesn't look pissed off, just confused.

"What are you doing?"

"I dunno." I shut off the phone. "Can't sleep."

"After the day we just had? Seriously?" Josh leans over and hits the light switch on the wall. The bare bulb above us flickers as it comes on.

"I have trouble sleeping sometimes. I get these nightmares. So it's just easier not to close my eyes, you know?" I try to laugh, make a joke of it. But Josh looks concerned. He looks like he's about to ask some questions. Questions I don't really want to answer. Then the light suddenly flicks off. The room goes pitch-black.

"What the hell?" I say.

"Shh—hear that?" Josh says.

I listen. A little wind outside, but otherwise completely silent.

"I don't hear anything."

"Exactly—the generator stopped." He's right. The deep thump of the generator has been a constant background noise at the resort all summer. Josh fumbles for his flashlight, then flicks it on. "Harvey might need some help restarting it. We should go."

By the time I'm at the door, Josh is still fumbling around with his clothes. "I'll go ahead," I say. He nods as he digs for socks under his bed, not looking at me. I hurry down the path toward the generator shack, the collar of my jacket up against the cold. A few snowflakes drift across my flashlight beam. Soon I come around a corner and see the shack. There's a blue light moving around inside it.

"Harvey?" I call out as I near the shack.

"Dylan?" Harvey opens the door, accidentally blinding me with his flashlight.

"Sorry about that." He points the flashlight down to the ground, and now I see his worried expression. "What are you doing out here?"

"I came to see if you needed help. Josh is on his way too." Harvey's eyebrows lift in surprise.

"Thanks. I appreciate that. But I don't think there's much any of us can do." He walks back into the shack, and I follow. My nose wrinkles against the acrid smell of scorched rubber. "A belt burned out. Snapped. I don't have any spares, so I'll have to drive into town in the morning." We leave the shack, Harvey locking it behind us.

"Get some extra blankets. It'll be a cold night," Harvey says. Then he crunches away up the path toward his cabin. I start to head off as well, my flashlight spilling a small pool of light on the ground in front of me. In the pale frost on the ground, I can follow my footprints back toward the Swamp. *Wait*. I stop and turn around, scanning the area.

Weird. There are my footprints. Then there are Harvey's, coming from the other direction.

And then, maybe, there's a third set. Fainter, more filled in with frost and snow. Another set of footprints leading to the shack. Me. Harvey. And who else? I crouch, trying to see where they come from. The snow is coming down faster now. Erasing everything.

"Dylan?" A beam of light spears into the darkness. It's Josh. I stand quickly and look down. There's no trace of anything, just a thin layer of snow.

"It's all over," I say. "We can go back to bed." On the way back to the Swamp, I keep my eyes on the ground. But I don't say anything to Josh.

Chapter Ten

Hours later, it's still dark outside. Josh and I are eating bowls of cold breakfast cereal in the Swamp when Harvey comes in. He's got a backpack slung over one shoulder and a gray wool hat tugged down over his wiry brown hair.

"I'm heading into town to get a new belt for the generator. I should be back before dinner. You guys work on the woodpile today. Get all the guest cabins stocked up, all right? Any problems, talk to Edward." We nod. He looks like he's going to say something else, but he just shakes his head and leaves. A minute later we hear a distant spray of gravel as the pickup roars up the road.

It's way colder today than yesterday. But pretty soon Josh and I end up taking off our jackets because we're sweating so much—this is hard work. Out at the woodpile, we fill two wheelbarrows with logs for the cabin fireplaces and guide them down the winding paths, trying not to tip over. Then we unload the logs in the cabins, stacking them neatly beside the stone fireplaces so that they're ready for next spring when the guests return.

It's about midmorning when I see the ravens. The big black birds are always around the place—it's called Raven's Lake for a reason. I normally don't pay any attention to them. But this is different. I drop the handles of my empty wheelbarrow and stare. I can see a big maple through the trees, a couple hundred feet away from the woodpile. It's a big old tree. Every branch is crowded with ravens, like black leaves on the bare, twisting branches. A swarm of them. And they aren't acting normal. They're standing still. All pointed in one direction.

Watching me.

I leave the path and crunch over the leaves toward the maple. I expect the ravens to startle and fly away. But they don't. Not until I'm right beside a group of ravens on the ground at the base of the tree. They hop back, cawing angrily at me, revealing what they have been pecking at. I catch a glimpse, then turn away, stomach heaving. I steady myself, then look back.

The mess of guts, blood and bone is barely recognizable as a raccoon.

A big one. It's been sliced up, almost turned inside out. Despite what the ravens have done to the body, I can tell that this wasn't really the work of wild animals. I've seen that before up here. This raccoon had clean cuts and incisions, reminding me of the dissections I had to do in high school. Puke rises again in the back my throat as I have a sudden thought—what if this is the raccoon we caught yesterday?

What if this is how Edward "took care" of it? I think of the bundle of knives on his bookshelf.

A sudden gust of wind shatters the flock of ravens above me. They take to the air, wheeling and turning. I stumble back to the path. I can see a hazy curtain of snow above the treetops, coming toward me. The wind keeps rising, and in a moment I'm surrounded by white. A snowstorm? This shouldn't happen for another month or so. The trees around me creak as the wind picks up speed.

"Josh?" I yell into my walkie-talkie. "Where are you?" I hear a crash way off in the woods. A tree coming down. I look up around me, searching for old branches that might fall. We need to get under cover.

"Josh?" I call again, but there's only the crackle of static in response. I leave the wheelbarrow behind. My head bent down against the wind, I cut across the grounds toward the main building. I stop when I hear something from the walkie-talkie. I press it against my ear. Static, then some words. Pineview, maybe? I turn and look toward the Pineview cabin, peering through the snow at it. Did Josh say he was in Pineview? I start toward the cabin, but a massive gust of wind forces me to look away and crouch. I hear a ripping sound. Louder than the wind. I look over just in time to see a tree topple. The roots tearing loose from the ground. The branches rushing through the air, gathering speed. Coming down and crushing the top of the Pineview cabin.

Chapter Eleven

I run toward the cabin. The huge fallen pine is cradled on the broken roof. Some of the branches have punched like spears through the windows. I peer through the snow for some sign of Josh. Then I see him running toward me from behind the cabin.

"Are you okay?" I shout over the wind. He leans toward me so I can hear him.

"Fine. I was out on the main path the whole time. I thought you were in Pineview when I saw the tree start to go. That's why I called you." Another huge burst of wind makes us both wince. "Let's get out of here!" We stumble through the snow toward the main hall.

When we get there, it takes some work to open the big door against the wind. Once it's closed, we both just rest for a second. Wet snow drips from our clothes onto the red carpet.

"I've never seen a storm like this," says Josh.

"You have not spent much time here," says a voice from behind us. I flinch. It's Edward, leaning against the frame of the door to his office, arms crossed. "It happens every few years. This is why you are working so hard to protect these buildings. The weather up here is destructive."

"Yeah, well, we just watched a tree come down on the Pineview cabin," I say. "It's still standing, but there's a lot of damage."

"I see," says Edward, straightening up. "Harvey will have to look at it when he returns. Come into my office."

We follow him inside. Edward turns to sit on the edge of his desk. Shadows flicker on the walls from the candles he has set around the room.

"I can see that you are both unnerved. The storm, the power failure—these are setbacks, to be sure." He looks so calm, so composed. Has he been hiding out here in his office the whole time? Doesn't he know what it's like out there? I look around his office. Maybe he does—the long winter jacket on the back of his door is wet, so he must have been out there recently. And there's something else. Something else in his office has changed.

"I don't think we should be out there," I say. Right away, I know I've said the wrong thing. It's like bait. Edward's eyes narrow.

"No, Dylan, 'out there' is exactly where you need to be," he says. He moves behind his desk, turning away and examining a candle on his bookshelf. "The weather is no excuse for being lazy. If anything, this storm gives you a reason to work more quickly." He carefully pulls some wax from the candle, not looking at us. "So back to work. I'll send Harvey out to look at the cabin when he returns."

I realize that I'm staring at an empty spot on his bookshelf. That's what's different.

The old knife roll. His black-cloth bundle of chef's knives. It was on the bookshelf last time I was here. It's gone.

It's as if there's a pressure wave building up in my head, and I can't hold it in anymore. I barely slept last night. All the weird stuff has been slowly cranking up the pressure in my head. And now it's going to burst out. I know I shouldn't say anything. That it will just make Edward mad. But the words tumble out of me.

"Edward, I want to leave. Like, right now," I say, my voice tight and angry. I walk around the desk until I'm standing right in front of him. I realize I'm shaking as I stare into his surprised face. I keep talking, faster and louder. "I think we all need to get out of here. There's no power, trees might come down on the road—or on the cabins. We could seriously get hurt. Or worse, like that kid who went missing a couple years ago. Right?" Edward looks deadly serious. But I stammer on. "Maybe we should just head into town and meet up with Harvey. Just take the other pickup and drive out. We need to get out."

I realize that I'm begging like a little kid, and I stop. Then there's just the sound of the wind rattling the windowpane. Even I know that I sound crazy. Like I'm totally losing it. I look at my hands. I'm still shaking. Maybe I *am* losing it. Finally Edward speaks.

"Have I not been clear?" he says. I expect him to be angry, so somehow it's worse when his voice is so calm and flat. Then it gets even creepier. He reaches over and gently brushes some melting snow from my red jacket. "My poor boy." He lifts one hand and gently cradles my cheek. But his expression hardens. "I have the only keys to the truck. We leave when I say we leave. And you work until I say that you stop. Am I not perfectly clear?" A thin slash of a smile creases his face. His eyes don't smile. "Do you need me to help clarify this for you?"

I flinch away from his cold fingers and shake my head.

Chapter Twelve

I slam open the heavy wooden door to the outside and keep moving. Josh runs to catch up to me as I walk quickly toward the Swamp. The snow is still coming down in thick curtains, but at least the wind is easing off. That will make what I'm about to do easier.

"Dylan, man, you okay?" Josh says. I don't answer, just keep crunching forward through the ankle-deep snow. "How about I make us something to eat? Sandwiches. We can sit down, talk things through."

I stop and face him. "Don't you get it? I'm done. I'm done with this place. I'm done with Edward." I fumble with my jacket zipper, trying to tug it farther closed. "I'm done with being scared all the time. Scared of going to sleep. Scared of what I might see when I'm awake," I say quietly. I give up on the zipper and keep walking up the hill.

"What are you talking about?" says Josh. We follow the path around a turn and head toward the Swamp. There are branches down all over the path, small ones torn loose by the wind.

"Since the start of this week, I can't sleep without having these nightmares. And then weird stuff keeps happening when I'm awake. Like out at the Point."

Josh stops me as I'm about to walk up the steps into the Swamp.

"Dylan, there was nobody there. It was just shadows or something," he says. He looks worried. Really worried. "You said it yourself—you haven't been sleeping. You've been acting kind of weird."

"*I'm* acting weird?" Unbelievable. "What about Edward? He's acting normal? The guy is dangerous!"

"He's mean. He's a bully. But he's… Edward, you know? We'll just stay out of his way until Harvey gets back. Do our jobs. Get paid."

I turn away from Josh and walk into the Swamp. A moment later, he follows me inside.

"Okay, what about the generator dying on us?" I ask as I pull out my backpack.

"The belt burned out, like Harvey said. What else would it be?" says Josh.

He sees me start putting clothes into the backpack. "What are you doing?"

"I'm going to walk to town."

Josh sits down heavily on his bunk.

"What? That really is insane. It's, like, two hours to drive to town," he says, "never mind walking in this storm."

"You don't get it. Things keep happening. The generator belt didn't just burn out. There were these foot-prints. And cabin seven. The way it was trashed. Those marks on the wall... it was something—"

"It was an animal that got in. Like that raccoon we caught." Josh watches me stuff a sweater into the backpack.

"Yeah, about that." I stop packing and face Josh. He looks really concerned. About me. That's when it hits me. It's all going to sound crazy. Even if I showed Josh the dead raccoon I found, what would I say? That a bunch of ravens led me to it? That I think Edward used his old chef's knives on it?

"Josh, listen." I put the backpack down on my bed. "I know this doesn't make any sense. But I need to leave. I can't stay here. I came up here to straighten out my head. But now it's making me crazy. Maybe literally." I shake my head and laugh a little. But it's not really funny. "You can come with me, or you can stay behind. Your choice."

"You're actually serious. You're going to walk out." After a moment, Josh shakes his head. "Just wait until Harvey comes back. He'll tell us what to do."

That's it, then. What am I going to do, carry him out? And for what? Maybe he's right. But I'm still feeling the rising panic that I felt in Edward's office. The pressure that keeps on building. The sense that something bad is happening all around me. I look at Josh, sitting on his bed with his pencil drawings pinned to the wall behind him. He's in a different world than me.

So in the end, I don't say a word to Josh. I just shrug the backpack onto my shoulders and head out the door. I stand on the path for a moment. Waiting to see if he'll follow me. But he doesn't.

I step off the path and head into the woods.

Chapter Thirteen

In the summer, I used to take my mountain bike out almost every day. A couple of the guys showed me where to find the old logging trails and deer paths. So I know that if I take this one path from the resort grounds, over a big hill, I'll come out on the main road and cut almost an hour off my walking time. It's midafternoon now, so I figure I can get at least three hours of walking in. That should get me to the highway, and from there I can hitch a ride to town. Josh was wrong, I tell myself. It's a solid plan.

Of course, in the summer the deer paths are a lot more obvious. My breath steams in front of me as I climb the gentle incline. The falling snow means I can't see more than ten feet around me. By the time I reach the crest of the hill, the wind has picked up again and reduced visibility even more. I start the descent toward the road, slipping a little on the loose snow. I grab hold of a tree to steady myself. Then, with a crack, the branch I'm hanging on to snaps. I wobble, the weight of my backpack throwing me forward. Before I know it, I'm crashing through the brush, rolling down the hill. I see a rock coming at me and try to protect my head with my arms. There's a flash of pain. Then darkness.

When I come around, I'm sure I've been out for just a couple of minutes. But when I look at the darkening sky, I realize it's been longer—closer to an hour. I'm wet and cold. I stand up slowly, feeling nauseous. Nothing is broken. But my head is pounding. I gently touch my forehead and wince in pain. No real blood. Just a big, swollen patch near my temple.

I look around, trying to get my bearings. The snow is still coming down, so I can't see where I fell from—everything is covered in a thick sheet of white. I'm starting to shiver with cold. Moving anywhere is better than staying put. I pick my direction and start walking toward the road. At least, I think it's toward the road.

A little while later, I'm less certain. It seems to be getting dark really fast. I stop and peer through the birch and pine trees. Trying to see past the screen of white snow. No sign of the road. I feel short of breath and nauseous again. What was I thinking, heading out into the forest on my own? I've got to find the road—otherwise I'm in serious trouble. My breathing is getting fast, ragged. I drop my backpack and frantically dig inside it. My phone. Maybe through some fluke, I'll get reception. Call for help. I stare at the little blue screen. Hoping.

Nothing.

It's when I look up from the phone that I see him. Red jacket like the employee one I'm wearing. Josh? He came after me! I start stumbling through the underbrush, yelling out his name. The snowfall thickens, and I lose sight of him for a second. When the snow stops, I find myself in a clearing. Alone.

"Josh!" I scream again and again, until my throat is hoarse and sore. Nothing. Did I go the wrong way?

I spin around, scanning the clearing and the trees beyond it. Nothing. Except— there, a flash of red under the snow near a big maple. I limp closer.

There's a small mound at the base of the old tree. I kneel down next to it and brush snow away from the little patch of red showing through. It's part of a jacket with the logo of Ravenslake Lodge. There's a name embroidered just below the logo—*Allen*. The rest of the jacket is buried under dirt and dried leaves. It's been here awhile. Carefully at first, then more forcefully, I push away the earth from the jacket. My gloves are torn and dirty, but I keep going, clawing at the cold dirt. Part of my mind is telling me to stop. Knowing what I'm going to find. Then my fingers touch something smooth and curved, and I see a fragment of white shining through the brown earth. A few more scoops with my hands, and I see it through the gathering darkness.

Bone.

The sweep of the brow. A hollow eye socket. Some teeth. A skull. I let out a strangled cry and fall backward. Scramble away from the thing in the snow.

Chapter Fourteen

I run across the clearing, half blind from the snow. From tears. Then I think I hear Josh's voice. I don't stop. I'm sick of imagining things. I'm not going to be fooled again.

So I almost run right into him. Josh. For real. Standing there in a big black parka, headlamp shining from out of his furry hood.

"Dylan! I thought I'd never find you, man. I've been out looking for ages. "I was about to give up." Chest heaving, I try to catch my breath.

"I need you to see something," I finally gasp. "I need someone else to see this. I need to make sure it's real."

Josh protests a little, but follows me back into the clearing. The skull is still there. He just keeps staring at it, framed in the circle of light from his headlamp.

"Is it…real?" he says.

"I think so."

"Who is it?" he whispers. "Who was it, I mean?"

"I don't know," I say. Then I remember what Tom said. About the kid who went missing. I tell Josh, and he nods hesitantly.

"I always thought that was just a story."

"Maybe not," I say. With the adrenaline dying away, my head starts throbbing badly. "We need to get out of here."

"Okay," says Josh. He shakes himself loose from looking at the skull and stares around the forest on the edge of the clearing. "We're actually pretty close to the road. The snow isn't falling much now. We should be able to follow my tracks back." He starts to trudge away and calls over his shoulder, "Don't get any crazy ideas about walking out to the highway tonight either. We have to go back to the lodge before it gets too cold."

"Wait, Josh," I say. He turns. "Thank you, man. I think you might have, you know, saved my life." Under his hood, even in the twilight, I can see him smile.

"We're even now."

He's right about the tracks. The snow has stopped falling, and the full moon even shines out occasionally through gaps in the clouds. It's pretty easy to follow Josh's footprints back to the road. The road itself, however, is in bad shape. We climb over a couple of big tree trunks that have been downed by the wind. I'm standing on top of one trunk, about to slide down the other side, when I realize what this means. Harvey isn't going to be able to bring the truck back. He's going to be stuck at the highway. I don't say anything about this, and neither does Josh. I think we both want to pretend that this isn't true. That Harvey is going to find some way to get back in here. And get us out.

It takes about two hours to walk to the Swamp, but it feels like we walked all night. Right away, I crawl into my sleeping bag, even though I'm wearing my clothes. I close my eyes. I feel like I could sleep for a week. Just as I'm drifting off, Josh nudges me.

"Shouldn't we go tell Edward about the…thing?" I open my eyelids, which feel like they're made of lead. He's staring down at me, worried.

"Yeah, I guess," I say. "Wait until I get a little rest, okay? I'm wrecked."

"What about your head? Shouldn't we get that checked out?" Josh asks. But I only hear him distantly, fading away, as I fall asleep.

The dream is different this time. It starts like a series of snapshots in black and white.

Raven's Lake. Still and calm. Empty except for the raft.

A tree full of black ravens, like black leaves clustered on the branches.

The Point. A shadow, someone on the edge of the campfire.

Cabin seven. The marks on the wall, deep gouges in the wood.

The skull, peering out from under dead leaves and dirt.

Then the dream snaps into motion, full color.

I'm underwater, and I think I'm going to be forced to watch my brother drown, again. But then I realize that this is different. I'm in the lake, diving down to save Josh. He's stuck on the bottom, feet tangled in weeds and mud. I pull myself down. Deeper into the water, reaching out for him. But when I see the red jacket, I realize it's not Josh. I swim closer and see rotting flesh. Decomposing skin. The corpse looks up at me and his lips move. I drift closer to him. And somehow, through the water, I hear his whisper.

"Seven."

Chapter Fifteen

I have to flick my lighter a few times before it catches. The candle slowly brightens. I bring it closer to Josh's bed.

"Wake up!" I hiss at Josh, shaking his shoulder. He looks confused. Fumbles for the glasses beside his bed.

"Why are you dressed?" he says. "What the hell are you doing?"

"We need to go to cabin seven," I say. "I need your help."

Josh sits up and rakes his hands through his long hair. "I thought we agreed. We'll wait until morning, then we'll go tell Edward and Harvey about the…body."

"You don't get it. Harvey isn't going make it back by morning. You saw the road, right? There are trees down all over the place. And you think Edward is going to help?"

With his round glasses and bed head, Josh looks like a flustered owl. He shakes his head slowly.

"I don't know," he says. "This is bigger than us. We need to tell someone."

"We can't trust Edward," I say. I lean in toward Josh and lower my voice. "And there's something else going on. I just saw something."

Josh looks uneasy. The candle flame flickers, then steadies.

"Saw something? When?"

"It's hard to explain." I rub a hand across my face. The headache is back, throbbing in my temple. "It was in this dream I just had."

Josh pushes his glasses up. Blinks a few times.

"You know how you sound, right? You don't trust anyone. Your dreams are telling you what to do."

"It's not like that."

"No, it's exactly like that. You need to get it together. You probably have a concussion or something from that fall. You're not thinking straight."

I turn away from him, furious. I shouldn't need his help. But the truth is that I'm scared. I'm scared of what I've seen. In real life and in my dreams. And after being alone in the woods, nearly dying out there, I don't want to go out alone. It's like I'm a little kid again. Scared of the dark.

I look at the black window, showing my pale reflection in the candlelight. I'm sick of being scared.

Maybe it's like my dad says—I'm making myself see scary stuff, when in fact there's nothing at all. I'm jumping at shadows. But I know there's something going on. And it's like I'm being shown a path and I have to walk down it. Maybe if I get to the end of the path, the bad stuff will stop.

"Stay here, then," I say. "I'll be back soon."

"Dylan," Josh says. "C'mon! What are you going to do? Get lost in the woods again? Be smart about this—" His words are cut off as the door slams behind me.

I pull up the hood of my jacket against the cold. Clouds have rolled in again across the sky. It's pitch-black as I walk through the cold night air to cabin seven.

I test the door—locked. Our keys don't unlock staff cabins, just guest cabins.

I slam my shoulder into the door. There's a sharp crack. The door swings open.

I walk into the cabin, playing my headlamp around the dark space. It looks the same as when I left it. A couple rows of bunk beds. An old bookshelf. Bathroom at the back. A woodstove in the center. I walk over to the marks on the wall and kneel down.

Deep gouges, all around that loose board. I remember thinking that Harvey would make us fix it up. I fumble around the board, testing, pushing. Nothing. I scan the cabin with my headlamp, my eyes finally settling on the woodstove. There's a long black iron rod—the fire poker. Perfect.

I shove the tip of the poker under the board and push down. Twice. Finally, it gives. I pull the board away from the wall just far enough to reach inside. My hand closes around something dry, soft, square. Papers?

I'm about to pull my hand out when I freeze. Over the low moan of the wind outside, I think I hear something. A slam. But then nothing else. Maybe it's just the wind knocking things around. I gently pull out what I've found in the wall. A small brown notebook.

I sit down on a bunk and carefully open it up. White pages covered in blue ballpoint pen. Sloppy handwriting, a little like mine. Dates at the top of each page—it's a diary. I flip back to the front cover. There's a name. *Allen Ender.*

Allen. The name on that scrap of jacket out in the woods. The name of the body. The guy who went missing.

I feel dizzy for a second. I feel that sense of pressure building up and up in my head. My hands start to shake, and I nearly drop the notebook on the floor. I take a deep, ragged breath and steady myself. I turn to the last pages of the diary. All these entries are dated October, after Allen had volunteered to stay on and close up the resort. One word keeps appearing on all these pages—*Edward*.

As I read, I realize that Allen had it even worse than Josh. Allen was alone up here that fall, just him and Edward. And Edward had decided that Allen was his personal project. Allen was a slacker who needed "training." He'd send Allen swimming out to the raft and back, just like he did with Josh. And other stuff. He'd wake Allen up in the middle of the night to carry wood to the cabins. Make Allen scrub the kitchen floors before he was allowed to eat. Cruel, petty stuff.

And Allen never fought back. Didn't seem to think he could. Thought that this was the way it had to be.

Even thought that he deserved it. That Edward was right about him, even as he seemed to get worse. The stuff Allen described was starting to sound more like abuse. Like torture.

I'm near the end of the diary when the writing stops abruptly. I turn the page, expecting to see more. But there's nothing. I flip to the end. Nothing. Just a couple of blank white pages.

I'm sitting there staring at the little book when I hear a noise behind me. I turn, automatically lifting my arm against the bright beams of two flash-lights. When my eyes adjust, I see Josh standing near the door of the cabin. Then Edward steps inside and rests a hand on his shoulder.

"You were right to come to me, Josh," says Edward. "Dylan is clearly not himself."

Chapter Sixteen

Edward crosses through the dark cabin until only a bed is between us. He shines his flashlight on the iron poker on the mattress. On the plank torn from the wall.

"More vandalism?" he says. "Disappointing. Harvey told me you had learned your lesson." He picks up the poker and moves to place it back next to the woodstove. "Clearly, you haven't learned a thing. We'll have to remedy that." My pulse is pounding. I look toward the door, but Edward turns suddenly, the poker still in his hand.

"Josh told me what you think you saw in the woods," he says, stepping closer to me. "You know, Josh says you've been seeing a lot of things recently. And that little wound on your head can't help. Must've been quite a fall." He reaches up with his free hand and brushes his fingers across the gash on my forehead. I flinch and catch sight of Josh. He blinks a few times and looks away.

"I had to tell him, Dylan," he says. "You were acting kind of crazy. I was worried about you."

My head throbs. Suddenly, I'm furious. Furious at Edward for what he did to Allen. To Josh. For what Edward's gotten away with all these years.

"It's not all in my head," I say, holding up the notebook. "This proves it. You remember Allen? He wrote all about you in here. All the crap you made him do. All the stuff you filled his head with." For once, Edward looks flustered. His mouth works, but nothing comes out. I keep going.

"What happened to Allen? He tried to run away, like me, didn't he? You kept on pushing him and pushing him until he couldn't take it anymore. Right?" Now I'm yelling. "Right?"

For a moment, standing there in the cold light of our flashlights, Edward is completely still. And pale. Like a corpse. Then his face wrinkles into a snarl.

"Not at all," he says. "Allen knew better than to try and leave. He was a smart boy. Not like you." Edward points the poker at me. "You just think you're smart. No, Allen was clever enough to always do what I asked." He steps even closer to me. His eyes have that look again—hungry, cold. Not quite human.

"But Allen, in the end, was too lazy." Edward snorts. "Like all of you, isn't it true? Why is that? All of you—slackers." He punctuates the word by tapping the poker on the mattress beside me. My back is against the wall. I look over at Josh. He's frozen, still near the door.

"So one morning, Allen just...gave up. And he had swum out to the raft so many times before. He was a strong boy. The cold shouldn't have been a problem. And yet..." Edward presses his face close to mine, close enough for me to gag on the metallic scent of his aftershave. "And I couldn't have questions, could I? Not everyone understands my training methods. It wasn't my fault that he was weak and couldn't make it back to shore. So I tucked him away in the woods. You understand, don't you, Josh?"

Edward suddenly turns toward Josh. I realize I've been holding my breath, and now I let it go. I slip the notebook into my pocket. We need to get out of here. I look around. There's only the one door. Where Josh is standing.

"Come here, Josh." Edward walks toward him, poker swinging at his side. "We'll start with you. We'll clean up this mess together, shall we?"

"What do you mean?" says Josh. He pushes his glasses back up on his nose.

"No!" I shout. Just before Edward swings the long iron poker at Josh's head.

Chapter Seventeen

As I stumble over the bunk, I hear the hollow thunk of the poker as it smashes into the doorframe. I lunge at Edward, hitting him in the lower back with my shoulder just as if this were a football game. He grunts and falls on his side.

"Come on!" I pull Josh outside. It's dawn, and the sky is lightening. But the wind and snow are swirling around us, making it hard to see. At first, I'm just running blind. Just trying to get away. I see the main hall in the distance. Maybe there's a door we can lock. A phone to call for help with. "This way!"

I look back and see Edward coming at us through the snow. Gaining ground. I grab Josh's arm again. He's panicking, stumbling. We hit the doors of the main hall, but they don't budge. Locked. I rattle them. They're too heavy to bust open.

"Around the corner," gasps Josh. "Loading dock." We run again, sliding on the snow-covered lawn. Up the steps leading to the rolling metal door. Josh shoves a hand into his jacket pocket and pulls out a ring of keys. I look over my shoulder as he rattles through them, trying to find the right one. No sign of Edward. Yet.

Josh finally finds the right key, and a moment later the rolling door clatters upward. We slip through and lock it down again. Then we both slump to the floor. The kitchen is still dark. Just a little gray dawn light seeps through the windows.

"We've got to find somewhere to hide," I say. I shine my headlamp around the kitchen, the light reflecting crazily off the stainless-steel counters. I stop at the big walk-in cooler. "What about that?"

Josh uses one of the keys to unlock the padlock on the handle. We push open the big door. There's a slight smell of something rotting—with the power outage, the temperature inside the cooler is the same as it is outside. Not great. But maybe we can hide in here for a minute. Figure out what to do. Josh goes in. I'm about to follow when I hear a noise. A door being unlocked. I click off my headlamp and crouch to the floor.

"Josh—stay quiet," I whisper. I hear muffled footsteps somewhere in the darkness. A flashlight beam wanders around the kitchen.

And finds me.

Chapter Eighteen

I stand and turn on my headlamp.
It's Edward. Flashlight in one hand.
A big chef's knife gleams in the other.

"As I said, Dylan," he says, "you're
not as smart as you think you are.
Not hard to figure out where you ran to.
So, where did the other one go?"

I realize I need to distract Edward
from the cooler. Give Josh a chance

to escape. "I don't know. He took off on me outside." I pull the notebook out of my pocket and put it on the silver countertop. "This is what you want though. Right? You can have it. And I'll never say a word. It'll stay a secret."

Edward looks amused. "That's very obliging of you. I have a better idea." He starts to walk toward me, down the aisle between the two counters. "Why don't we go visit Allen again? I'm sure you will be good at keeping secrets. Just like he is."

Before he can reach me, I leap and slide over the countertop, barely landing on my feet. I run for the loading-dock door and start to heave it up. I feel a sharp pain on my shoulder and realize as I tumble through the opening that Edward's knife must have made contact. Adrenaline keeps the pain down though. I jump down the steps and run. Anywhere. Away.

Through the snow swirling around me, I hear the sound of waves. I veer toward the dock—maybe I can get to the boat. Get away from shore before Edward catches up with me. I hit the dock and skid on the icy wood. I scramble back onto my feet. The inflatable is still in the water. Still no gas tank, but I don't care. I lower myself into the rocking boat. Fumbling with the icy ropes, I try to untie the bowline. I'm almost finished when a boot stamps down on my hand. I cry out.

"Dylan. Shame on you," Edward says, panting. "Adding theft to your list of crimes?" He reaches down and tries to grab my wrist, but I pull my throbbing hand away and fall backward in the boat.

"You have so much room for improvement. Let's get you back up here." We stare at each other for a moment—Edward, wild-eyed and sweaty, looking down on me from the dock, me flat on my back on the floor of the inflatable. I can feel the cold water through the thin hull of the boat.

"Come up here now," he commands. "Don't make me come after you."

I shake my head. He yells in frustration. Paces up and down the dock like an animal at the zoo. The big knife in his hand looks dull and gray in the pale morning light.

"All right, then. I will come to you," he says. Still pointing the knife at me, he clumsily starts to lower himself off the icy dock and into the boat. I shrink back toward the end of the inflatable. Trying to get away from him. Knowing that there's nowhere left to go.

Just as Edward extends one leg into the boat, I see a shadow rise up behind him.

Josh.

He lets out a wild yell as he shoves Edward from behind. Pushes him hard toward the water. Edward's arms flail as he goes down. He lands hard on the edge of the boat, pushing it down into the water. I try desperately to hold on to the boat as it rises up.

But then the boat flips completely over, and the icy black water rushes around me.

Chapter Nineteen

I'm not sure if this is a dream or not. I can't tell anymore.

I'm in the lake. Surrounded by icy water. I can see the murky shape of Edward in front of me. The knife falls from his hand, shining weakly as it spins away. Edward is trying to swim back up toward the surface. Then I see another shadow, reaching up out of the darkness. An arm covered in the tatters of a red jacket.

Allen.

One shadowy hand grips onto Edward's ankle. For a moment, Edward keeps trying to swim upward. Then he looks down. He silently screams as those dead hands slowly pull him deeper and deeper. Until he fades from sight into the blackness beneath my feet.

I look up at the shiny surface of the water above me. The pounding in my head fades, all pain drifting away.

I can't make it back up.

And you know what? I'm okay with that. I'm tired. Of the nightmares. Of being afraid of what I might see. Of feeling guilty. I just want to let it go. Let it all go. I'll be like Sammy now. Forever looking up at the light.

Then I feel something wrap around my chest. Two small arms. Another shadow.

Not Allen. Sammy. I can't see his face in the gloomy dark, but I know that it's him. Telling me that it wasn't my fault. That it's not my time. Not yet.

Then the brightness is just above me, and the small dark shadow lets go. Sammy drops back into the darkness. I want to hold on to him, for just a little longer.

I puncture the surface. Air rushes into my lungs. Then Josh is hauling me onto the snowy dock.

I lie there for a while, sobbing. Not just because of the pain and fear, but because I can let go. Let Sammy go.

I'm alive.

Chapter Twenty

I remember one thing from what happened next.

It took Harvey one more night to reach us. Part of it was the freak storm, which kept sending out wave after wave of wind and snow. But even when the storm subsided, he and some volunteers had to chainsaw their way through all the fallen trees on the road.

I don't remember the waiting. I don't remember how we survived.

Harvey finally found Josh and I huddled around the fireplace of a guest cabin. He told me later that we were lucky. I was in shock from exposure and the loss of blood from the wound in my shoulder. Josh wasn't in much better shape after diving in to get me out of the water.

I don't remember trying to explain about Edward to Harvey. About the skull in the woods. The ghosts. The body. Harvey says it took awhile to calm me down. That he nearly had to carry me to the pickup to get me to the hospital.

So here's the one thing I remember.

Driving down the road in the back-seat of Harvey's pickup. Away from Ravenslake Lodge. Wrapped in blankets. Feeling safe for the first time in a long time. Watching the forest of white birches blur past the window.

Thousands of pale trees fading away into the distance.

And then, from the corner of my eye, something red. Someone. Or something. Watching me leave.

I keep telling myself that ghosts don't exist. That I'm only scaring myself. That it's all in my mind.

But I don't really believe it anymore.

Sean Rodman lives and works in Victoria, British Columbia. His interest in writing for teenagers came out of working at some interesting schools around the world. In the Snowy Mountains of Australia, he taught ancient history to future Olympic athletes. Closer to home, he worked with students from more than a hundred countries at a nonprofit international school. For more information, visit www.srodman.com.

Gypsum Public Library
P.O. Box 979 52 Lundgren Blvd.
Gypsum, CO 81037
(970) 524-5080

Gypsum Public Library
P.O. Box 979
Gypsum, CO
(970) 524-5080

W9-CQS-971

S c o t t   T r a v e r s'
Top 88 Coins Over $100

44-Coin Hot List • 44-Coin Blacklist
By Scott A. Travers

Foreword by Q. David Bowers
Introduction by Ed Reiter

Copyright © 1998 by Scott A. Travers
All rights reserved

Except for appropriate use in critical reviews or works of scholarship, the reproduc-
tion or use of this work in any form or by any electronic, mechnical or other means
now known or hereafter invented, including photocopying and recording, and in any
information storage and retrieval system is forbidden without the permission of the
publisher.

Library of Congress Cataloging-in-Publication
Travers, Scott A.
Travers' top 88 coins over $100: 44 coin hot list, 44 coin blacklist
     p.   cm.
ISBN 1-56625-0104-4
1. Coins, American — Collectors and collecting — Handbook, manuals, etc. 2. Coins
as an investment — Handbooks, manuals, etc.
I. Title.
CJ1832.T74 1998   98-39729
332.63 — dc21   CIP

Bonus Books, Inc.
160 East Illinois Street
Chicago, Illinois 60611

First Edition

Printed in the United States of America

Author Inquiries:
Scott A. Travers
P.O. Box 1711
F.D.R. Station
New York, NY 10150-1711
Tel: 212-535-9135
Fax: 212-535-9138
E-mail: travers@inch.com

Table of Contents

Two winners on the cover: An 1804 Draped Bust silver dollar (left) which sold at public aution for $1,815,000 and a 1913 Liberty Head nickel which sold at public auction for $1,485,000. Both coins were sold by Bowers and Merena of Wolfeboro, New Hampshire, on behalf of Louis E. Eliasberg Sr., a Baltimore banker who formed the only complete date-and-mint collection of all U.S. coins.

COVER PHOTOGRAPHS COURTESY AUCTIONS BY BOWERS AND MERENA.

Acknowledgments

T he author was assisted in preparing this book by a number of highly knowledgeable individuals who generously shared their expertise. I wish to extend my gratitude to: John Albanese, Q. David Bowers, James E. Brandt, Helen L. Carmody, John W. Dannreuther, Thomas K. DeLorey, Silvano DiGenova, Michael R. Fuljenz, David L. Ganz, Larry Gentile Sr., Salvatore Germano, David Hall, David C. Harper, John Highfill, Steve Ivy, Robert W. Julian, Chris Karstedt, Kevin J. Lipton, Raymond N. Merena, James L. Miller, Lee Minshull, Martin Paul, Donn Pearlman, Ed Reiter, Maurice H. Rosen, Will Rossman, Michael Keith Ruben, Margo Russell, Florence M. Schook, David Sundman, Anthony J. Swiatek, Mark Yaffe and Keith M. Zaner.

Ed Reiter rendered particularly valuable service in editing the text, drawing upon his extensive background as a numismatic journalist, including nearly a decade as Numismatics columnist of *The New York Times* and more than a dozen years as senior editor of *COINage*.

Bowers and Merena Galleries provided not only astute market insights but also large numbers of exceptionally high-quality photographs to accompany the text. Special thanks go to Doug Plasencia, the company's talented photographer, for his work on the illustrations.

And accolades also go to Chris Karstedt, the firm's marketing director, for her diligent attention to detail on many aspects of this project.

Foreword

Winners and losers. Losers and winners. An interesting concept, indeed. While the idea seems simple at first glance, a little double-thinking can produce some very interesting results.

If a coin is a "loser" market-wise, and the price is in the cellar, is it a loser for *you*? Maybe yes, maybe no. Certainly it was a loser for its past owner, if he or she bought it at a market high point and sold it at a low point. But, if now is that low point, perhaps this loser of yesterday can be the winner of tomorrow. Such things are interesting to contemplate, and in this new book, Scott Travers certainly provides some interesting food for thought.

As in any other walk of life, opinions in numismatics are diverse. I might think that a sparkling little copper-nickel Civil War token from 1863, depicting an Indian Head on the obverse with the quaint legend "The Prairie Flower," is a dandy thing to buy, a joy to own. On the other hand, you might say, "Who would want such an obscure item? Why, it is not even listed in the *Guide Book*, and how the heck can I find its market price each week?"

Turning to the specifics of the moment, I like Trade dollars from 1873-1883, and I agree with Scott that these are true winners. However, I cannot help but notice that a Proof-64 at $2,500 is only *half* the price of a Proof-65, yet it is apt to be only slightly *lower* in grade! Lots of value here, in my opinion. The point is that even within the recommendations Scott gives, there may be some hidden values worth investigating.

As to the "loser" 1881-S Morgan dollar, in my opinion the advanced numismatist will not do a headstand when seeing a gem MS-66 specimen offered for $155. However, for John Q. Public, who may never have seen an old and interesting silver dollar before, this coin may be a great introduction to numismatics and monetary Americana. Just because it is common doesn't mean that it is not desirable.

This brings up another point: A coin may be a loser in one way and a winner in another. Scott's book will prompt you to *think*. Agree with his conclusions, or disagree if you wish. No matter, you've been stimulated to investigate further. Scott mentions the 1950-D nickel. Now there's a classic *loser*. However, one might think that at $300 per roll, or less than eight dollars per coin, these might be a good value in 1998. Who knows?

Like the hand of cards in Kenny Rogers' *Gambler* song, every coin has something to like and something to dislike. Actually, most of the coins Scott lists have something basic to like — about the design, their place in history, etc. It seems that the *market performance and price* are the focal points for liking and disliking.

Look over his listings. Read his ideas. Then make your own choices. Scott prompted me to do some thinking of my own. My gosh, there are some good buys out there. (Check out the 1913-S Type II Buffalo nickel, one of my favorites.) Have fun!

Q. David Bowers
Numismatic scholar and author
of dozens of books on rare coins

INTRODUCTION

Everyone loves a winner — and everyone loves to win. Successful sports teams draw more fans than perennial also-rans. Best-selling authors get higher advances and bigger promotional budgets than struggling neophytes. Blue-chip stocks with proven track records attract more investors than marginal performers.

Football coach Vince Lombardi liked to say that "winning isn't everything — it's the only thing." That absolutist approach may be better suited to professional athletics than to everyday life, but few would dispute that winning is better than losing. And that is surely true when it comes to buying rare coins — or, for that matter, any coins for which the seller charges you a premium.

COINS AND COLLECTING

Coin collecting is probably almost as old as coins themselves — and those date back more than two-and-a-half millennia, all the way to the seventh century B.C., when the first rudimentary coins appeared in the small Asia Minor kingdom of Lydia. Those earliest coins were crude pieces of gold and silver alloy stamped with a simple design — the head of a lion, for instance — to denote their official status.

For centuries, only men of wealth had the time and

resources needed to pursue, procure and preserve rare coins. Indeed, this came to be known as "The Hobby of Kings." As the modern era brought redistribution of wealth and greater leisure time for increasing numbers of people, coin collecting attracted an ever-growing army of new recruits. Ironically, it enjoyed a period of major expansion during the Great Depression — a time when few people had any money to spare, much less to save. Spurred by the introduction of inexpensive "coin boards," many Americans started devoting part of their newly enforced spare time to assembling sets of cents and other low-value coins from pocket change.

By the late 1950s, millions of Americans had extra cash to go with their extra time, and many began investing large sums of both in what had now become "The King of Hobbies." Much of the money was misdirected at first into rolls and even bags of mint-state modern coins; by their very nature, these were relatively common and had limited potential to appreciate in value as collectibles. The roll craze began to fizzle in the early 1960s, and the focus then turned instead to high-grade examples of individual coins — lower-mintage coins from the nation's earlier years. By the early 1980s, this new approach had developed a tremendous head of steam — fueled, in large part, by the marketing of coins to a new breed of buyer: the "investor." And the emphasis on quality had led to the creation of numerical grading standards to pinpoint the condition of coins — and, by extension, their current market value — with unprecedented accuracy.

THE ELEMENTS OF VALUE

Having written newspaper and magazine columns about the coin hobby for nearly three decades, I can state unequivocally that when it comes to coins in their possession, most people have one overriding concern: What's it worth? Thus, when we speak of coins as "winners" or "losers," we are referring inevitably to their present market value and, even more importantly, the potential they possess to increase in value in years to come.

The value of a coin as a collectible is based upon three principal elements: supply (or rarity), demand and quality. Think of them, if you will, as the legs of a tripod supporting the price of that coin in the rare-coin marketplace.

• The very term *rare coin* underscores the importance of rarity — small supply — in establishing how much a coin is worth. To justify the payment of a premium above and beyond — often far beyond — face value, a coin must have limited availability. If there are enough examples to go around, there's no incentive to pay a special premium. Official mintage figures are obvious yardsticks of rarity, but these are not always indicative of the actual number available. Precious-metal coins may have suffered attrition through melting, for example. And some coins may be scarcer in pristine mint condition than their mintages suggest, either because they were not well struck to begin with or because they were never saved in significant numbers.

• Demand is the counterpoint to supply. A coin can have a very low mintage, in absolute terms, and yet not command an especially high premium if its base of potential buyers is also small. Conversely, a coin with a large collector base can bring a sizable premium even if its mintage isn't minuscule. Lincoln cents, for instance, appeal to many collectors — so even though the 1909-S VDB Lincoln cent has a mintage of nearly half a million, it's still highly prized and quite high-priced. Combine high demand with low supply and you will be blessed with perfect harmony — the kind that makes beautiful music, and hits all the high notes, on a well-tuned cash register.

• Quality has become an ever more important determinant of value as the coin market has evolved and matured in recent years. This is due, in part, to the mind-set of the investors who entered the market in large numbers — and spent vast sums of money on coins — during the 1970s and, to an even greater extent, the 1980s. Unlike traditional collectors, who tended to stress rarity over quality and frequently were satisfied with less-than-prime condition, many of the investors equated high quality with high value, drawing upon their experience in other areas. This, in turn, led dealers to cater to this taste by seeking out high-grade coins (often without much regard to their rarity), featuring them in their inventories — and, of course, boosting their prices to reflect the new reality of growing investor demand.

INDEPENDENT THIRD-PARTY GRADING

The emphasis on quality led to urgent calls for uniform grading standards, a call that was answered by the American Numismatic Association (ANA), the national coin club, in the late 1970s when it formulated a grading scale using the numbers 1 through 70, with 1 representing a coin that was barely identifiable and 70 denoting a coin that was absolutely flawless. The ANA Certification Service began grading coins according to these standards in 1979, and initially buyers and sellers responded enthusiastically. Within a few years, however, dissatisfaction developed regarding the accuracy and consistency of the grading. Among other things, many critics complained that the ANA graders were not market-wise, as coin dealers are, and thus were applying the standards in an academic manner, rather than in a commercial way.

David Hall, one of the nation's best-known and most innovative coin dealers, brought order from this growing chaos in 1986 when he assembled a high-powered group of other leading dealers and founded a new company called the Professional Coin Grading Service (PCGS). This visionary company introduced a practice known as *consensus grading*, whereby each coin submitted for review underwent inspection by at least three different graders and their individual assessments then were combined in a single consensus grade. It also introduced a practice that came to be known far and wide as coin *slabbing*. After its grade was determined, each coin examined by PCGS was encapsulated in a hard, sonically sealed plastic holder, along with a small tab designating its grade and other pertinent information. This not only averted possible tampering with the grading tab, but also protected the coin from deterioration.

The Grading Revolution had begun, and PCGS was soon being hailed as the savior of the 1980s coin boom. One of the company's founding dealers, John Albanese, left a short time later to form a competing service called the Numismatic Guaranty Corporation of America (NGC). In the intervening years, both companies have prospered, and between them they have certified millions of coins — lending stability to the marketplace and shoring up buyer confidence that had started sagging noticeably prior to their appearance on the scene.

Unless noted otherwise, the grades discussed in this book are those assigned by either PCGS or NGC. "Raw" or uncertified coins trade at a discount, as a rule, because of uncertainty regarding the grades the services would assign to them if they were submitted for certification. There are other grading services — notably ANACS, the successor firm to the ANA service, which is now owned by Amos Press, the publisher of the weekly hobby newspaper *Coin World*. These companies have their niche and their grading is professional, but the Big Two enjoy greater marketplace acceptance.

THE AGE OF TYPE COINS

Years ago, the typical collector assembled U.S. coins in sets, seeking out one example of every date in a series from every mint that struck the coin that year. This is know as "date-and-mint" collecting. This approach made sense at a time when most coins were inexpensive — or could be obtained directly from circulation without paying anything extra at all. In recent years, date-and-mint collecting has become too costly for many collectors. Coins that used to be readily affordable now carry big premiums in many cases.

As a result, many collectors content themselves today with what are known as *type sets*. Rather than pursuing every single coin in a given series, they settle for just one coin and let that represent the entire series. But, since they are limiting themselves to only that single coin, they look for an exceptional example — generally selecting a high-grade, mint-state specimen of a common-date coin in the series, since that will be less expensive than a similar example of a scarcer-date piece.

Even though PCGS takes up much of his time these days, David Hall remains an active participant in the marketplace — and is still among the most astute observers and analysts of the numismatic scene. Hall considers Mint State-65 type coins to be tremendous winners; in fact, he regards them as some of the biggest winners in the market at this time — primarily because the emphasis on type collecting heightens the demand for these coins, and is likely to continue doing so for many years to come. Among his favorite series are two-cent pieces, silver three-cent pieces, Capped Bust quarter dollars, Liberty Seated quarters and Trade dollars.

WINNERS AND LOSERS

Vince Lombardi, to the contrary, winning and losing aren't necessarily absolute. They can come in degrees and nuances, rather than being strictly black and white. Many times, for instance, a coin may be a winner at one price but a loser if you add, say, 20 percent — not so very much, really — to that price. Or a coin graded Mint State-64 may be a winner while its counterpart in Mint-State-65 — just one level higher on the 1-to-70 scale — may be a loser. Today's winner could be tomorrow's loser if market conditions shift even moderately. Then again, some winners — and some losers — may retain those designations for the rest of their lives and ours.

There is one absolute winner associated with this book, and that is its author. Based on a professional and personal association dating back nearly 20 years, I can vouch without reservation for the intelligence, independence and integrity of Scott A. Travers. He is not only the most knowledgeable person I have encountered in the coin field, but also the most reputable. And unlike some experts I have encountered over the years, Scott willingly and enthusiastically shares his deep knowledge — not only through his books and magazine and newspaper articles, but also though frequent appearances at coin shows and other public forums, invariably at his own expense. Years ago, I described him in a *New York Times* column as "the Ralph Nader of numismatics," and this title is just as warranted now as it was the day I coined it. Scott watches over the interests of the little guy and — despite admonitions from those who fear adverse consequences for their own self-interest — he points out the perils and pitfalls year in and year out, steering the unwary from the many traps that lurk in this complicated marketplace.

Scott Travers' Top 88 Coins Over $100 is yet another service to the hobby — and specifically to the little guy who needs help in steering clear of trouble. It isn't all-inclusive; no single book could possibly cover the subject comprehensively. But it highlights the things to look for — as well as the things to avoid. And while it doesn't color every nuance in vivid detail, it paints the broad outline so clearly and dramatically that readers cannot fail to get the picture.

Read this book closely and you'll get a new perspective on what really counts when you buy and sell coins. Follow the recommendations embodied in these pages and you'll be well on the way to being a winner yourself!

Ed Reiter
Former Numismatics Columnist
The New York Times

Photo courtesy of Bowers and Merena.

W I N N E R   N O .   1

Trade dollars
graded Proof-64 or 65

n 1873, Congress passed far-reaching legislation that had a profound effect on U.S. coinage. Among other things, the legislation authorized a new silver coin slightly heavier than the standard silver dollar and containing slightly more precious metal. This coin, called the Trade dollar, was meant to give U.S. businessmen an advantage in their dealings with Asian merchants, especially the Chinese.

Besides producing this coin in a business-strike version for use in overseas trade, the U.S. Mint also made small quantities of proofs every year for sale to the nation's collectors. These sales were quite modest, reflecting the fact that relatively few Americans collected coins in earnest at that time. In the thirteen-year history of the Trade dollar, the number of proofs exceeded 1,000 in only four different years.

This odd silver coin never really achieved its objective as a vehicle for international trade, and after just six years its production for that purpose was suspended. The Mint continued to issue proof specimens, though, from 1879 to 1885 before retiring the coin altogether. In the final two years, the numbers it made were minuscule — ten in 1884

Photo courtesy of Bowers and Merena.

and a mere five in 1885. These, of course, are great rarities and command enormous premiums, putting them beyond the reach of the typical coin buyer. The other Trade dollar proofs are far more available and affordable, but nonetheless qualify as legitimately rare coins, with mintages ranging from a low of 510 in 1877 to a high of 1,987 in 1880. Considering how elusive they are, they represent good values at current market levels — about $2,500 in Proof-64 and $5,500 in Proof-65. They are rare, beautiful, old, historic and desirable.

L O S E R   N O .   1

Generic Morgan dollars
graded Mint State-65, 66 or 67

Morgan silver dollars hold great appeal for investors. They're also special favorites of dealers who cater to investors. There are several good reasons for this appeal. For one thing, Morgan dollars are large silver coins that exude a combination of heft and intrinsic value. For another, they are the numismatic equivalent of antiques, dating back to the 19th century in most cases — yet, many millions are preserved in mint condition. They represent a link to America's Old West. And, in a number of instances, they are legitimately scarce and valuable as collectibles.

But not all Morgan dollars are truly scarce, even in pristine mint condition. Some of them, on the contrary, are readily available in high Mint State grades — available by the thousands even in such a lofty grade as Mint State-66. That's because vast quantities of these cartwheels never saw use in commerce; after being minted, they sat for generations in bank or government vaults. Consider the 1881-S Morgan, a coin of which the San Francisco Mint struck 12.76 million examples. As of January 1998, the Professional Coin Grading Service and the Numismatic Guaranty Corporation of America had certified a combined total of 10,243 of these coins as MS-66 and 1,417 as MS-67.

The 1881-S dollar was exceptionally well struck and remains extremely attractive more than a century later. But with so many specimens readily available, is it really worth $155 in MS-66 and $435 in MS-67 — the prices being quoted as this is written? And does it have good potential to soar in value? Probably not, because many thousands more exist, ready to be certified in equally high grades, increasing the supply even more. This is what is known as a "generic" coin, relatively common even in superb condition. Don't be blinded by the dazzle of this and similar coins; you'll be paying for the sizzle, not the steak.

Photo courtesy of Bowers and Merena.

W I N N E R   N O .   2

Lafayette dollars
graded Mint State-63

France played a pivotal role in helping the American colonists win their independence from Great Britain, and no single Frenchman was more crucial in that effort than the Marquis de Lafayette. France had not yet entered the American Revolution when the wealthy young nobleman — then just nineteen years old — sailed to Philadelphia in 1777 to join the Colonial army. Quickly gaining the confidence of General George Washington, he was appointed a major general and fought with distinction through the end of the war, despite being wounded in the Battle of Brandywine.

In 1899, on the eve of the 1900 World's Fair in Paris, American admirers came up with the idea of erecting a statue in that city in Lafayette's honor as a gift to France. To help raise funds for the project, the Lafayette Memorial Commission petitioned Congress to authorize production of 100,000 commemorative half dollars, which it then could sell at a premium. Congress instead authorized 50,000 silver dollars, which were offered for sale for $2 each.

The Lafayette dollar is a fascinating coin. It was the first U.S. commemorative silver dollar — and the only one from

Photo courtesy of Bowers and Merena.

the "traditional" period of U.S. commemorative coinage. It was the first legal-tender U.S. coin to portray a real-life American (George Washington, who is shown in profile along with Lafayette). And, though it is dated 1900, its entire mintage was produced on a single day, December 14, 1899 — the 100th anniversary of Washington's death. Only 36,000 examples of the coin were distributed, the rest being melted years later, and many of these saw circulation. As a result, relatively few examples exist in mint condition, making this a scarce and coveted rarity with a strong collector base. I especially recommend it in Mint State-63, a grade in which this coin is aesthetically pleasing and eminently collectible without being inordinately expensive. At present, it is priced at about $1,100 in this grade. The combined NGC and PCGS population figure for this coin in MS-63 is 645 pieces.

LOSER NO. 2

Iowa commemorative half dollars graded Mint State-65

Commemorative coinage, like proof coins and other frills, spent World War II on the sidelines while the U.S. Mint focused all its efforts on meeting the demand for coinage of the realm. The program was suspended in 1939 and didn't resume until 1946, when

Congress authorized a special half dollar to celebrate the centennial of Iowa's admission to the Union. It turned out to be one of only three new commemorative coins issued by the U.S. Mint during the postwar period.

The Iowa half dollar wasn't the highest-mintage coin from the so-called "traditional" period of U.S. commemoratives, which stretched from 1892 to 1954. A number of other issues had higher production figures than this coin's 100,000. But unlike many of those others, the Iowa's net population wasn't reduced by large-scale melting; no unsold coins were returned to the Mint, so all 100,000 (or virtually all, at least) remained available. Furthermore, Iowa halves tend to be sharply struck and problem-free, so many have been certified as Mint State-65. As of January 1998, the Professional Coin Grading Service and the Numismatic Guaranty Corporation of America had certified a combined total of about 10,000 Iowa half dollars — 3,680 of them as Mint State-65.

What worries some observers isn't that so many Iowa halves have been "slabbed" by the grading services, but rather that so many more remain to be certified in the future. Approximately 90 percent of the total mintage hasn't been submitted to the certifiers yet, and this serves as a huge overhang — and a potentially serious depressant on the current market value of about $100 in Mint State-65. There's a lot of corn in Iowa — and a lot of Iowa coins.

WINNER NO. 3

1971 Eisenhower dollars graded Mint State-66

Dwight D. Eisenhower first won fame as a military hero. He assured himself a prominent place in American history by skillfully directing the D-Day invasion of Normandy, France — the event that turned the tide once and for all in World War II, putting the United States and its allies firmly on the road to ultimate victory. But Eisenhower was destined for even greater glory: In 1952, he sought election as the nation's 34th president, and won in a landslide. He went on to serve two full terms, firmly stamping the 1950s as "the Eisenhower years."

When Eisenhower died in 1969 at the age of 78, numerous suggestions were made for memorial tributes. One such proposal was to issue a coin in his honor. The idea appealed to President Richard Nixon, who had been vice president under "Ike," and he lent his support to it from the White House. Reluctant to displace any of the five presidents from the nation's existing coins, Congress resurrected the dollar denomination, which had not been issued since 1935. The Eisenhower dollar was introduced in 1971 and struck for the final time in 1978.

Unlike previous U.S. dollar coins, the circulating version of the "Ike dollar" contained no precious metal, being made instead of two outer layers of copper-nickel alloy bonded to a core of pure copper — the same composition used in current dimes, quarters and half dollars. The coin proved difficult to mint with sharp detail and most specimens were poorly struck, particularly in the early years. Furthermore, collectors perceived the new dollar as worthless and thus set aside few examples. As a result, exceptional specimens from

1971, the first year of issue, are few and far between — and well worth the premium of $400 or more in Mint State-66 condition. They have marvelous potential to bring four-figure prices in years to come.

LOSER NO. 3

A complete set of Eisenhower dollars, proof and uncirculated, in typical condition

As of this writing, some dealers are advertising complete sets of Eisenhower dollars for not much more than $100. These sets include all the proofs, plus all the business-strike pieces in mint condition. This sounds like a pretty good deal — for even though this series lasted just eight years, you're getting more than two dozen coins, they're all brand new and some of them contain precious metal (a reduced silver content of 40 percent). Actually, it isn't the worst deal in the world. But it's also far from the best, for the Eisenhower dollars found in most such sets are commonplace and unlikely to appreciate significantly in value.

Although they are extremely scarce and potentially quite valuable in very high levels of preservation, Eisenhower dollars are readily available — and worth little or nothing above face value — in typical uncirculated condition. Hundreds of millions were minted and many of these, while technically uncirculated, are aesthetically unappealing. They're weakly struck, bag-marked, lacking in luster and, all in all, rather ugly. These are the kinds of coins that often end up in ready-made sets. Ike dollars also are common in proof, and while a Mint State-67 piece could be worth a pretty penny, a Proof-67 example probably would bring only a nominal premium. The bottom line is, you're paying $100 or more for coins that are available by the millions in a set that has minimal intrinsic value and almost no potential to rise in value as a collectible.

Rather than spending $125 or $150 for an entire set of common Ike dollars, you'd be better off to spend a little more and get a single coin in Mint State-66. That's where the potential for future gain exists. Remember, though, that the earlier dates are scarcest in pristine mint condition — and the coins to buy are the business strikes, not the proofs.

Photo courtesy of Bowers and Merena.

WINNER NO. 4

The 1792 half disme

The coin we call the "nickel" is such a familiar part of our lives that we hardly ever give it a second look — or a second thought. We don't stop to question why it's so much larger than the dime, a coin with twice the value. Or why it's called a "nickel" when its composition is actually 75-percent copper and only 25-percent nickel. It would come as a great surprise to most Americans to learn that for three-quarters of a century, the U.S. Mint didn't even produce such a coin, and people made do instead with a small silver five-cent piece called the "half dime."

As its name suggests, the half dime was precisely half the weight of the dime and the same metallic composition — a more logical arrangement (although a less practical one) than what we have today. The nickel five-cent piece proved more convenient and therefore more popular when it was introduced in 1866, and the half dime was abolished seven years later. But when it first appeared, the small silver coin saw widespread use in commerce and suited our forefathers' taste for coinage with high intrinsic value.

The very first half dime is looked upon by many as the first U.S. coin of any kind. It was struck in the cellar of a Philadelphia home in July 1792 — months before the opening of the nation's first mint in that city. Notwithstanding the location, the 1,500 pieces made at that time had congressional authorization. What's more, they were minted from silverplate provided by President George Washington. These coins bear the inscription HALF DISME, "disme" being French for "tenth" (as in tenth of a dollar). The Mint later anglicized this to "dime." The 1792 half disme is rare, historic and desirable — and while it will cost you thousands of dollars even in circulated condition, this is a coin that will always be in great demand.

LOSER NO. 4

Proof-67 war nickels

I n 1942, the United States was climbing a steep, treacherous hill as it battled from behind in World War II. The effort required total dedication by the American people and affected all aspects of daily life, including the nation's coinage. Nickel was critically needed for war-related uses, so in 1942 the U.S. Mint changed the composition of the five-cent piece, removing nickel and instead making the coin from an alloy of copper, silver and manganese.

Wartime austerity also led the Mint to suspend production of proof coins for the duration of the campaign. It did make these collector coins in 1942, though — including some Jefferson nickels of the regular composition (75-percent copper and 25-percent nickel) and some with the substitute alloy. In all, it produced 57,200 proof five-cent pieces dated 1942, of which 27,600 — slightly less than half — were "war nickels."

Over the years, promoters have hyped these proof war nickels and driven up their prices. Just a few years ago, a Proof-65 example would have cost you $350. But when the promotions ended, the prices plummeted, and as of this writing in early 1998, that same coin can be had for just $50, and a Proof-67 specimen for $350. Does that mean these nickels are bargains? On the contrary, it underscores how volatile and risky the market is. While 27,600 is clearly a modest mintage by present-day standards for U.S. proof coins, which routinely are made by the millions, these coins are far from rare. In fact, the U.S. Mint made more proof nickels in 1942 than in any other year before 1950. And many of them exist in Proof-67. True, another promotion could push prices up again temporarily — but when it comes to war-nickel proofs, I'd be gun-shy.

Photo courtesy of Bowers and Merena.

W I N N E R   N O .   5

The 1856 Flying Eagle cent in Proof-63, 64 or 65

The Lincoln cent has been around so long that most of us can't imagine life without it; introduced in 1909, it has outlasted the vast majority of the U.S. population alive at that time. The cent hasn't always carried Abraham Lincoln's portrait, though. In fact, it hasn't always been the size it is today. For more than sixty years, from the start of U.S. coinage to the eve of the Civil War, the cent was a large, bulky coin — almost the size of today's half dollar — and was made not of bronze, brass or copper-plated zinc, like most Lincoln cents, but rather of pure copper.

By the 1850s, the large copper cent had worn out its welcome — along with the pockets of many Americans — because it was so heavy and inconvenient to carry around. The U.S. Mint conducted tests to find a suitable substitute and settled at length on a much smaller coin made from an alloy of 88-percent copper and 12-percent nickel. The coin was the same diameter as the current Lincoln cent but thicker and nearly twice as heavy, and, because it carried a portrait showing an eagle in flight, it came to be known as the Flying Eagle cent.

The Flying Eagle cent wasn't struck for commerce until 1857. However, the Mint produced small quantities of the coin in 1856 for presentation to members of Congress, Treasury officials and other dignitaries, partly to show them what it had in mind and partly to win their support. Researchers estimate that more than 600 were distributed in this fashion and that hundreds of restrikes were made a few years later, using the same dies, for sale to collectors of the day — a combined total of possibly 1,500, all of them proofs. The 1856 Flying Eagle cent has always been popular with collectors and doubtless always will be. Besides being rare, it's also the nation's first small-size cent. Prices are far from cheap — $6,000 in Proof-63, $8,000 in Proof-64 and $15,000 in Proof-65 — but this coin will always be worth a pretty penny.

L O S E R   N O .   5

An uncirculated roll of 1950-D Jefferson nickels

At first glance, the 1950-D Jefferson nickel appears to be a real bargain. Its mintage of just over 2.6 million is the lowest in the entire Jefferson series, a series that dates back to 1938. And as of early 1998, a roll of forty uncirculated 1950-D nickels was retailing for less than $300 — a small fraction of what it would have brought in the early 1960s, when the market value peaked at $1,200 per roll.

The fact is, however, that even at such a seemingly depressed price level, a roll of 1950-D nickels is no bargain. True, the mintage is low, at least by the standards of this series — but collectors were aware of this at the time the coin was issued, so they hoarded rolls and even bags of this nickel. As a consequence, a very high percentage of the 2.6 million examples ended up being preserved in mint condition. It may very well be, in fact, that this coin is scarcer in circulated condition than it is brand new.

In all likelihood, the 1950-D nickel is more common in mint condition than numerous other Jeffersons from around the same period whose mintages are considerably higher, since those coins weren't set aside to nearly the same extent when they were new. There is serious doubt whether it even merits its current market value of roughly $7 per coin. And purchasing it in roll quantities makes little sense, for that just multiplies the potential overpayment forty times. Buying rolls of uncirculated late-date coins was all the rage in the early 1960s, but that approach has been discredited by their generally dismal performance during the intervening years.

Photo courtesy of Bowers and Merena.

WINNER NO. 6

The 1926-S Buffalo nickel graded Mint State-64

Everybody loves the Buffalo nickel. This ruggedly handsome coin is pure Americana — the very embodiment of America's frontier past and the rough-and-tumble, romanticized era that saw this nation fulfil its "manifest destiny." Collectors are no exceptions: Few, if any, U.S. coins enjoy such a solid base of dedicated enthusiasts.

Oddly, the most expensive coins in this series are offbeat varieties, rather than standard date-and-mint issues. The 1916 nickel with a doubled-die obverse and the 1918-D overdate, with the 8 engraved over a 7, both command five-figure prices in mint condition. The 1937-D "three-legged" nickel, with a missing foreleg on the bison, isn't far behind on the price charts. The standard issues do have their share of scarce and desirable collectibles, however. The three most challenging coins in this group are low-mintage nickels struck in the 1920s in San Francisco: the 1921-S, 1924-S and 1926-S. And of these three, the 1926-S is head and shoulders — plus tail and haunches — above the rest.

To start with, the 1926-S is the lowest-mintage coin in the Buffalo nickel series (not counting oddball varieties). At 970,000, it's the only coin in the series with a mintage below

1 million. And, to compound its rarity, it's notorious for being weakly struck. Sharply struck examples are few and far between — and when they do turn up, they bring impressive premiums. You'd be hard-pressed to find an example of this date in grades of Mint State-65 and above, and you'd have to pay dearly to obtain one. Even in Mint State-64, the price is hardly cheap: upwards of $3,000. That would be money well spent, though, for when you combine the great popularity of Buffalo nickels in general with the genuine rarity of the 1926-S, and then add attractive mint condition, you have a sure-fire formula for future appreciation.

L O S E R N O. 6

The 1938-D Buffalo nickel graded Mint State-67

Appearances can be deceiving. The 1938-D Buffalo nickel is a classic case in point. At first glance, this coin seems to be the numismatic equivalent of the guy who has everything: Its mintage is relatively low, at just over 7 million; it's almost always sharply struck and aesthetically appealing, even dazzling; and it's part of a coinage series that perennially ranks as one of the most popular — more than that, one of the most beloved — in all of American history. Despite all these positive attributes, though, this is one of the lowest-priced coins in the Buffalo nickel series. Its value is so modest, in fact, that you have to go all the way up the scale to Mint State-67 — what some describe as a "super-grade" coin — before its price tag tops $100.

It must perplex the uninitiated to look at a price list and see the 1938-D Buffalo running neck and neck with the 1936, a nickel whose mintage of 119 million is 14 times higher. The puzzlement can only be compounded by the fact that a number of Buffalos with comparably low mintages

— the 1919-D, 1919-S, 1920-D and 1925-S, for example — bring much higher premiums right across the board than the 1938-D, particularly in pristine mint condition.

In a sense, what we have here is too much of a good thing. Unlike the earlier branch-mint nickels I just mentioned, the 1938-D was set aside by collectors in very substantial quantities immediately after its release. In large part, that's because this was the final coin in the Buffalo series; the Jefferson nickel took its place later the same year, and widespread publicity about the impending change had alerted the nation's hobbyists — and non-collectors, too — and prompted many to save both kinds by the roll and even the bag. Also, while its sharpness makes the 1938-D more attractive than many earlier branch-mint Buffalos, it also makes the coin readily available in even the highest grades — and under the law of supply and demand, that depresses its value. Some of the earlier coins are impossible to find with razor-sharp strikes; by contrast, the 1938-D is almost impossible to find *without* such a strike. Given all this, I'd steer clear of the 1938-D. That MS-67 piece really isn't a bargain at $125. There are just too many fish in this particular sea — or rather, too many bisons on this plain. The combined NGC and PCGS population figure for this coin in MS-63 is 958 coins as of January 1998.

Photo courtesy of Bowers and Merena.

W I N N E R   N O .   7

The 1955 doubled-die Lincoln cent graded Mint State-63

E verybody makes mistakes, and the U.S. Mint is no exception. Despite its determined efforts at quality control, the Mint produces coins with obvious imperfections now and then — and though it catches many of these before they get away, others find their way into general circulation and end up as intriguing conversation pieces. They also end up as coveted collectibles, avidly pursued by a large and growing body of "error-coin" enthusiasts nationwide.

One of the biggest "boo-boos" ever to escape from Uncle Sam's clutches was a 1955 Lincoln cent with dramatically doubled images on the date and the inscriptions on the obverse. This error came about because of misalignment in a process known as "hubbing" of the dies. A coin is created by striking a planchet, a blank piece of metal, with two dies— one bearing the design for the obverse, the other having the elements for the reverse. On each die, the design appears in mirror image. A die, in turn, is made by striking a piece of tempered steel with a hub — a harder piece of steel on which the design is positive, or just the way it will look on the finished coin. To make the impression stronger, technicians give each master die multiple blows with the hub. On rare occasions, the hub and die become misaligned between blows — and when that happens, the die emerges with doubling of the images. That's what happened in 1955.

Inspectors discovered this problem, but not before small but significant quantities of "doubled-die"cents — perhaps 30,000 — had been mixed with normal coins. Rather than destroy the whole batch, they decided to let the misstrikes go. This was a bonanza for collectors, for the coins soon became sought-after prizes. Most entered circulation, however briefly, and mint-state examples are extremely scarce. Given this small supply and the great demand for these coins, they're well worth the going price of $1,200 in Mint State-63. They have nowhere to go but up.

LOSER NO. 7

The 1995 doubled-die Lincoln cent graded Mint State-67

Collectors across the country got out their magnifying glasses in the spring of 1995 when they learned of an exciting new discovery: Brand-new Lincoln cents dated 1995 were turning up with doubling on the obverse, or "heads" side. It wasn't as sharp and obvious as some of the earlier "doubled-die" errors had been, but it was clear enough — especially when viewed under even low-power magnification. The doubling was most apparent on the letters of the word LIBERTY.

Reports about these coins soon began appearing not only in hobby newspapers and magazines but also in general-interest periodicals. Most impressively, *USA Today* ran a story and a photograph on its front page. The treasure hunt was on — and many of the treasure hunters ended up hitting paydirt as they looked through bags and rolls of uncirculated cents. The 1995 doubled-die cent wasn't as dramatic as its 1955 and 1972 counterparts, but it seemed to have been struck in much more meaningful numbers and distributed much more widely.

This was a good-news, bad-news situation. The coin's availability made it easier for hobbyists to find one in circulation and add it to their collections for an outlay of just one cent. On the other hand, it exerted increasingly downward pressure on the value of the coin as the law of supply and demand took effect. Typical examples of the coin, grading perhaps Mint State-63, had been selling for about $200 apiece in the beginning, but ended up being worth less than $25. As this is written, MS-67 pieces still carry a price tag above $100 — but given the extent of the supply, I would not buy one at that level. The price almost surely is headed even lower.

Photo courtesy of Bowers and Merena.

W I N N E R   N O .   8

The 1913-S Variety 2 Buffalo nickel graded Mint State-64

The winning of America's Old West was a saga that combined triumph and tragedy. One of its greatest tragedies was the slaughter of the vast herds of American bison — popularly known as buffalo — that had roamed the Western range just a few decades earlier. Those herds were decimated by white settlers, who killed the animals for food, clothing, and sometimes just for sport. In 1850, it was estimated that 20 million head of buffalo populated the Western plains; by 1894, the number was barely 1,000. This loss was keenly felt by many Americans, and the buffalo came to symbolize the passing of an era in the West. This admiration, in turn, helped make the Buffalo nickel an immensely popular coin when the U.S. Mint introduced it in 1913.

The very first examples of this chiseled-looking coin were different from those that followed in a subtle yet significant way: The bison was depicted standing atop raised ground — what collectors refer to as a "mound." This reinforced the naturalistic appearance of the coin. Unfortunately, though, designer James Earle Fraser had chosen this location for the crucial inscription FIVE CENTS — and because this part of the coin was relatively

Photo courtesy of Bowers and Merena.

high and exposed, that statement of value soon began wearing off in circulation. To correct this problem, the Mint did away with the mound, showing the bison instead on a straight line or "plain," with the words FIVE CENTS recessed below it.

Buffalo nickels were made in both varieties that year at all three mints then in operation — Philadelphia, Denver and San Francisco. The scarcest of these was the "plain" variety from San Francisco, with a mintage of barely 1.2 million. The S-mint "mound" variety also is scarce, with a mintage of only about 2.1 million. But this was saved in far greater numbers in mint condition because it was the first to appear; when the second version came out, many saw no reason to set it aside. The 1913-S Variety 2 nickel is far from cheap; in Mint State-64, it will cost you roughly $900. It's worth the money, though, for it's extremely elusive in higher grades.

L O S E R   N O .   8

The 1913 Variety 1 Buffalo nickel graded Mint State-66

The "mound"-type Buffalo nickel has much to recommend it. To begin with, it's a one-year type coin; only the very first coins in this series — those produced in the early months of 1913 — show the bison (or "buffalo") standing atop raised ground. By April of that year, Mint officials realized that the words FIVE CENTS — engraved on the mound — were wearing off quickly in circulation, and moved to correct this by leveling the surface underneath the buffalo and recessing, and protecting, the statement of value. Beyond that, the so-called Variety 1 nickels possess a rough-hewn surface that is missing on subsequent pieces, and many collectors consider them aesthetically more appealing. Mint technicians needlessly smoothed out the design's details at the same time they were making the needed modification of the mound.

Given all this, one might assume that Variety 1 Buffalos would command hefty premiums. This assumption would seem even safer upon examination of the coins' mintage figures, for these are only marginally higher than those of the "plain"-type nickels of 1913. At the Philadelphia Mint, for example, production levels were virtually the same for the two varieties: not quite 31 million nickels with the mound, and not quite 30 million with the straight line under the buffalo.

In point of fact, however, Variety 1 nickels are far more available in pristine mint condition than those of Variety 2. That's because they came out first, so they were the ones most people set aside as mementos. By the time the modified version appeared, the Buffalo nickel had been around for months and people were getting used to it, so the novelty — like the inscription — was wearing off. The modification is meaningful to collectors, but it held no special significance to many in the non-collecting public. Variety 1 Buffalos are certainly desirable, especially in high levels of preservation, but you must be careful not to overpay for them. The going price of $150 for the Philadelphia nickel in Mint State-66 strikes me as too high for a coin that is really not so scarce. As of January 1998, the combined population number for this coin in MS-66 graded by NGC and PCGS was 1,135 pieces.

Photo courtesy of Bowers and Merena.

WINNER NO. 9

Proof State nickel three-cent pieces

The U.S. coinage lineup is highly compact today. Even with the addition of a new dollar coin in the year 2000, the nation is entering the new millennium with just six different circulating coin denominations — and one of those, the half dollar, sees little or no use in circulation. By contrast, Americans had more than a dozen coins at their disposal during much of the 19th century — including different coins of the same denomination. For a brief period after the Civil War, the U.S. Mint was making two different kinds of five-cent pieces (one in nickel, the other in silver), two different three-cent pieces (also in nickel and silver) and two different dollar coins (in gold and silver, respectively).

Today, it seems odd to think of having a three-cent piece at all, much less two kinds. This curious denomination first came into being in 1851, when the Mint began producing the silver version — a small, wafer-thin coin intended to simplify the purchase of postage stamps, whose basic rate was then being lowered from five cents to three. The silver three-cent piece proved impractical, though, because of its tiny size — and in 1865, under pressure from nickel-mining interests, Congress approved a new kind made of 75-percent copper and 25-percent nickel —

Photo courtesy of Bowers and Merena.

the same alloy used in the Jefferson nickel today.

The nickel three-cent piece never was widely used in circulation, but it did serve a purpose by helping the federal government retire the unpopular three-cent fractional notes issued as emergency money during the Civil War. The coin was discontinued in 1889, after more than a decade of generally very low mintages. But, while the public may not have embraced it at the time, many current collectors find the coin desirable — especially in mint condition and proof. The Mint struck proofs, or specimen coins, each year of the series' life — nearly half of them in quantities of 1,000 or less. I particularly like them in Proof-66. The going price for such a coin is a mere $700, and is more than justified by the rarity.

L O S E R   N O .   9

Mercury dimes from the 1940s graded Mint State-67 with full split bands

Coin collectors have gotten very fussy in recent years. Whereas previous generations of hobbyists were satisfied, for the most part, with problem-free, lightly circulated coins, many collectors today will settle for nothing less than mint condition. Some insist on pristine mint condition, and pay substantial premiums for the privilege of owning very high-grade coins. In some cases, this is justified because the coins in question are rare or extremely scarce in such condition. In other cases, however, substantial numbers exist in grades above Mint State-65, so disproportionate premiums are unwarranted.

One of the byproducts of quality consciousness has been a heavy emphasis on whether certain coins are sharply struck in designated areas. These are areas that normally exhibit weakness — so if they are fully struck, the coins are deemed to be superior examples and often command impressive premiums. For instance, Miss Liberty's head tends to be weakly struck on Standing Liberty quarters, so "full-head" examples are highly prized and often very high-priced.

Over the years, collectors have observed that Winged Liberty (or "Mercury") dimes have weakness, as a rule, in portions of the fasces on the reverse. This device — a symbol of authority in Roman times — consists of a bundle of rods bound around an ax, and by rights there should be separation in the bands that bind the bundle. But only the sharpest specimens possess this separation, so "full-bands" Mercury dimes are looked upon as scarce and worth a premium. Beware of paying big premiums, though, for full-split-bands dimes from the 1940s. Unlike earlier issues, many of these were sharply struck, so the premium — if any — should be nominal. The current price of $150 for MS-67 examples with full split bands is excessive. The 1944-D in MS-67 with full split bands, just one coin, has a combined total population from NGC and PCGS of 968 pieces.

Photo courtesy of Bowers and Merena.

WINNER NO. 10

The 1909-S Lincoln cent graded Extremely Fine or better

The Lincoln cent is taken for granted today by most Americans. But when it first appeared in 1909, it was really quite revolutionary: Up to that time, no U.S. coin minted for use in commerce ever had portrayed a real-life person from the nation's past. The coin was conceived as a tribute to Abraham Lincoln on the 100th anniversary of his birth, and while its simple portrait may seem commonplace today, in 1909 it represented a breakthrough artistically, as well, for up to then U.S. coinage had been heavily allegorical. This cent, by contrast, was handsomely realistic.

When coin collectors think of the very first Lincoln cents, they tend to focus on those bearing the letters "VDB." The coin's designer, Victor David Brenner, had placed those letters — which are his initials — at the base of the reverse as a kind of artistic signature. It is common practice for coin designers' initials to appear on their creations; James Longacre's "L" can be found on the bonnet ribbon on the Indian Head cent, for example, and Charles Barber's "B" is etched on Miss Liberty's shoulder on the Barber silver coins. But those are rather small and inconspicuous. Brenner's three initials seemed to jump right off the coin, prompting public

Photo courtesy of Bowers and Merena.

protest and leading to their removal soon after production got under way.

The San Francisco Mint had struck only 484,000 Lincoln cents before the initials were removed. The 1909-S VDB cent turned out to be the lowest-mintage coin in the whole Lincoln series, not counting errors and varieties, and has been a prized collectible ever since. The West Coast mint went on to produce 1,825,000 cents without the designer's initials in 1909 — and while these are far less publicized, they're still extremely scarce and desirable. You can expect to pay about $100 for a 1909-S cent graded Extremely Fine, and several times as much for one that is Mint State-63, but this is a scarce issue in a highly popular series — even without the VDB.

L O S E R   N O .   1 0

The 1931-S Lincoln cent graded Mint State-65

"Brother, Can You Spare a Dime?" That became the theme song of the Great Depression for millions of Americans who found themselves with no jobs, no money and little or no hope that prosperity — or even recovery — would really be around the next corner. Hardly anyone had a dime to spare, or even a red cent —

including the United States Mint, where production fell to its lowest ebb in the 20th century. The Mint made gold coins every year till 1933, but few of those were distributed, much less used. Other than those, the Mint issued only cents, nickels and dimes in 1931, cents and quarters in 1932 and cents and half dollars in 1933. New coins were super-fluous at a time when so many people couldn't afford to spend them.

Lincoln cents were minted every year, but at very low levels. Production hit rock-bottom at the San Francisco Mint in 1931, when just 866,000 cents were struck all year long. That's the second-lowest mintage of any Lincoln cent, not counting errors and varieties — topped (or rather, bottomed) only by the 1909-S VDB, whose output totaled just 484,000. But whereas the 1909-S VDB circulated widely, and thus is extremely scarce in mint condition, the 1931-S saw little or no use in commerce. The lack of demand for circulating coinage was one obvious reason. Beyond that, however, the coin's low mintage became common knowl-edge among collectors, and much of the supply was set aside before it even entered circulation. One old-time dealer reported being offered a chance to buy nearly half the total mintage — some 500,000 pieces — at one time from a Western bank.

The 1931-S cent carries a price tag of nearly $200 in Mint State-65, and the figure gets rather fancy in grades above that. Thousands and thousands exist in mint condi-tion, however, so you should be wary of paying a big premi-um for this coin. It's a classic case where despite a low mintage, the available supply is still quite ample.

Photo courtesy of Bowers and Merena.

WINNER NO. 11

Type 3 Liberty double eagles graded Proof-65

David Hall, the highly astute founder of the Professional Coin Grading Service, commented once that "only real men collect proof gold." His point was that proof U.S. gold coins are rare and expensive right across the board, so only people with lots of buying power — and the willingness to risk large sums of money — can afford to dabble, much less take a full-scale plunge, in this high-stakes corner of the marketplace. Every proof gold coin is, quite literally, a trophy to be cherished and savored.

Proof gold coins are dazzling in any denomination — but because of their size and heft, proof double eagles (or $20 gold pieces) represent the ultimate in mint-making magnificence. These large, heavy coins contain very nearly an ounce of gold and, being proofs, they are superior — sometimes superb — specimens both technically and aesthetically.

Saint-Gaudens double eagles get the most attention, but I have always been partial to the Liberty gold $20s that preceded "Saints" in the U.S. coinage lineup. These elegant-looking coins are rooted in the mid-19th century, and their issuance spanned a period of more than half a century during which the nation fought and survived a bloody civil war, won the American West and literally expanded from sea to shining sea. Collectors divide Liberty $20s into three types: from 1849 to 1866, the coins lacked the motto IN GOD WE TRUST; the motto then appeared until the end of the series in 1907; and from 1877 till the end, the statement of value was shown as TWENTY DOLLARS, rather than TWEN-TY D. This last group, known as Type 3, is the one I especially recommend. A Proof-65 example will cost you about $20,000, but, with mintages ranging from a low of 20 to a high of just 158, these coins are not only dazzling but downright rare. Real men — and women — will always desire them.

L O S E R   N O .   1 1

An uncirculated roll of
1960 small-date Lincoln cents

Lincoln cents have always been enormously popular with collectors. Their low face value makes it extremely affordable for even the youngest collectors — armed with just a modest weekly allowance — to collect them from circulation. Plus, scarcer-date issues and interesting varieties can — and do — turn up in pocket change. Back in 1960, the U.S. Mint produced a Lincoln cent that combined these two elements: a scarce coin that was also an interesting variety. And it touched off a treasure hunt that brought many thousands of brand-new collectors into the hobby.

That coin was the 1960 small-date cent.

Normally, the Mint changes just one number — the last one — on the master dies for its coins at the start of each calendar year. But once every ten years, at the start of a new decade, it has to change the second-to-the-last number, as well. That's what happened in 1960. Soon after the start of production, Mint technicians noticed that the numbers on the new cents were becoming clogged. To correct the problem, they made the numbers larger. In doing so, they unwittingly created a scarce and popular variety: As collectors soon discovered, the early strikes — those with a "small" date — were readily distinguishable from the later ones, and a great deal harder to find.

Small-date cents were made at both mints then in operation, Philadelphia and Denver, but those from the former were particularly elusive. Researchers estimate that no more than a few million examples were produced there — and at one time, these were selling for $400 or more per roll of fifty uncirculated pieces. As this is written, the price is just about $100 per roll, and I see little likelihood that it will rise significantly in the foreseeable future. This is an interesting variety, and many collectors include it in their Lincoln cent collections — but while it's scarce, it's available. And virtually every example was saved in mint condition without ever reaching circulation, so there's little or no premium on high quality.

Photo courtesy of Bowers and Merena.

WINNER NO. 12

A 1936 Walking Liberty half dollar graded Proof-65

Whenever collectors and connoisseurs of coinage art draw up lists of America's loveliest coins, the Walking Liberty half dollar never fails to rank among their top selections. This stunningly beautiful coin is truly a numismatic masterpiece, and many observers place it at or near the top of their lists, along with the Saint-Gaudens double eagle. The United States Mint apparently agrees, for in 1986 it chose the obverse portrait from the Walking Liberty coin, with its full-length view of Miss Liberty, for the obverse of the American Eagle silver bullion coin. The Saint-Gaudens design was chosen for the gold American Eagle, so this was a powerful statement that in the government's view, the "Walker" stands at the head of the class among U.S. silver coins, just as the exquisite "Saint" does among the gold.

The magnificence of the design is shown to greatest advantage on proof specimens, where multiple striking captures each delicate detail and subtle nuance, and where there is maximum contrast between the frosty devices (or raised design areas) and the highly polished fields (or background portions). Proof Walking Liberty halves are among the most breathtaking coins Uncle Sam ever made.

Photo courtesy of Bowers and Merena.

Although the series lasted for more than three decades, from 1916 through 1947, proofs were struck for public sale in only seven years — from 1936 through 1942. And while the number of proofs was modest throughout that span, it was easily the lowest in 1936, when the Mint produced just 3,901. You'll pay a pretty penny for the privilege of owning one: In Proof-65, this coin carries a price tag of about $2,000. But you'll have a coin possessing exceptional beauty, extremely high quality and very low mintage — a rare combination indeed.

LOSER NO. 12

Common-date Walking Liberty half dollars graded Mint State-66 or 67

Rarity and quality are attributes that enhance the value of a coin as a collectible. They might be described as twin towers. When a coin possesses both of these characteristics, its value can be very great indeed. When it possesses neither, its value is likely to be relatively small. But what about a coin that has one of these two attributes, but lacks the other? Determining the value of such a mixed-bag coin can require specialized knowledge, broad experience — and, most important of all, common sense.

Complicating matters is a factor that is called "condition

rarity." Certain coins are common in circulated condition, or even lower levels of mint condition, but scarce or even rare in very high levels of preservation. This is true, for instance, of some coins in the Morgan dollar series. Take the 1886-O silver dollar, for example. This coin has a mintage of more than 10 million and is readily available in circulated condition. Its value soars, however, in mint condition — and especially in grades of Mint State-63 and above.

This brings us to another popular U.S. silver coin — the Walking Liberty half dollar. The lowest-mintage coins in this series — the three half dollars of 1921, the 1916, the 1916-S with the mint mark on the obverse and the 1938-D — command a meaningful premium, a premium based on rarity, even in lower grades. Some of the coins with somewhat higher mintages command significant premiums in the higher grades — this time because of condition rarity. Relatively few exist in such high grades. In both of these examples, the premiums are justified. All too often, though, dealers put high price tags on common-date Walking halves based entirely on their quality, even though rarity — and even condition rarity — doesn't exist. Many of these coins, especially those from the later years in the series, are really quite abundant even in grades as high as Mint State-66 or 67. Don't let their pretty faces fool you — and don't pay their fancy prices.

Photo courtesy of Bowers and Merena.

WINNER NO. 13

Franklin half dollars
graded Mint State-66 or Proof-66 or higher

The Franklin half dollar first appeared on the scene at about the same time as the "baby-boom" generation of Americans. And under normal circumstances, it — like the baby boomers — still might be a highly visible part of the scene today. Events conspired, however, to cut short the life of this interesting coin after only fifteen years of production.

Under legislation enacted in 1890, regular-issue U.S. coins (the kind meant for use in everyday circulation) can't be replaced until they have been minted for at least twenty-five years. But Congress has the power to override this law if it so chooses — and that's what it opted to do during the closing days of 1963. Emotions were high following the assassination of President John F. Kennedy on November 22 of that year, and sentiment was strong to honor the slain president on a U.S. coin. For various reasons, Congress selected the half dollar as the vehicle — so the Franklin half dollar, introduced in 1948, suffered a premature death a decade before the coin would have reached the statutory minimum age. Even then, existing Franklin halves normally would have lingered in circulation for many years, but in 1965, when the Mint began producing "clad" cupro-nickel coins, older silver coins quickly disappeared into hoarders' hands.

There are no major rarities in the Franklin half dollar series — at least not in terms of the quantities made; the lowest-mintage issues, the Philadelphia halves of 1953 and 1955, both were minted in numbers approaching 3 million. But specialists have discovered that many Franklin halves are extremely hard to find — sometimes almost impossible — in very high grades with full, sharp strikes. The design is deceptively simple, with Benjamin Franklin's portrait and the likeness of the Liberty Bell both having clean, open looks. But subtle details are missing from most of these coins, even in mint condition; few, for example, display full lines on the bell. Franklin half dollars are common in grades of Mint State-63, Proof-63 and below; in higher grades, however, they command substantial premiums, generally much more than $100 — and based on their scarcity, they're well worth it.

LOSER NO. 13

A Susan B. Anthony dollar graded Proof-69

The Susan B. Anthony dollar is a quintessential "loser" — perhaps the biggest loser in the annals of U.S. coinage. This singularly unloved and unlamented coin was conceived as a convenience for American consumers: It gave them a small-size, high-value coin for use in such devices as vending machines, pay phones and toll-collection baskets — or so the reasoning went. At the same time, it had the potential to make a small fortune for Uncle Sam. That's because each "Susie" cost just pennies to produce, but went on the books as a dollar when it entered circulation, giving the federal government a profit of roughly ninety-seven cents per coin in what is known as "seigniorage."

In theory, it couldn't miss. But in practice, this coin —

with its curiously ugly portrait of suffragette Anthony — was a failure from the outset. People found it aesthetically unattractive; saw no reason to switch to this newfangled coin from good old dollar bills; and, most telling of all, had a hard time distinguishing it from the only slightly smaller Washington quarter. Besides being close in size to the 25-cent piece, the Anthony dollar also had the same composition and thus the same physical appearance. Anybody who spent one in place of a quarter, thereby incurring a 75-cent loss, became an unremitting enemy of the coin.

Unpopularity notwithstanding, certain Anthony dollars do command premiums in some dealers' price sheets. Proof-69 specimens, for example, appear in occasional ads with price tags well above $100. Ostensibly, this is because Susies are hard to come by in very high grades. It's true they're not abundant in Proof-69 — but they're also not rare. Proof Anthony dollars tend to be decently struck, and many — indeed, most — have survived in their original state of preservation because they were issued in highly protective packaging. All in all, they're just more losers.

Photo courtesy of Bowers and Merena.

WINNER NO. 14

Mint State Capped Bust dimes

Age is relative. To most present-day Americans, movies, songs — and yes, U.S. coins — from before World War II seem old and dated. They are, after all, six decades or more in the past, and sixty years in human terms would represent very close to a full lifetime. Those same prewar coins look a lot more modern, though — a lot more up-to-date — when viewed alongside such truly old coins as Capped Bust U.S. dimes from the early 1800s. Those coins predate not only World War II but also the Civil War — and, for that matter, the Mexican-American War.

The dime was among the basic denominations authorized by Congress in the Mint Act of 1792. However, it was among the last of those coins to enter production, not being issued until 1796. The earliest dimes were slightly larger and heavier than their modern counterparts, and were made from an alloy containing slightly less than 90-percent silver; since 1965, dimes have been devoid of precious metal. The very first dimes had what is known as a "Draped Bust" design, showing a bust of Miss Liberty with drapery over her shoulder. In 1809, the year of Abraham Lincoln's birth, this portrait was modified and a turban-type cap was placed on Liberty's head, creating what is known as the Capped Bust dime. This design continued until 1837, when the coin's dimensions were slenderized, giving it the diameter still in use today.

Capped Bust dimes had extremely low mintages, judged by current standards. In only four years did their output exceed 1 million — and then not by much. Furthermore, there were nine years when the total came to less than 500,000. Moreover, few were saved, since coin collectors were similarly sparse in those early years. You can expect to spend close to $1,000 even for a specimen graded just Mint State-60, and several times as much for one that grades MS-63. But these coins are legitimately scarce and well worth the premiums they bring.

LOSER NO. 14

A complete set of U.S. Olympic coins from any given year

More than a century has passed since the modern Olympic Games took place for the very first time in 1896 in Athens, Greece. During that time, the Games have evolved into a global extravaganza — a spectacle that serves as a showcase and a springboard for the greatest amateur athletes in the world and, at the same time, cloaks their athletic achievements in a mantle of national pride. Today, there are Olympics every two years, with Summer Games and Winter Games both on four-year timetables in alternating even-numbered years.

Initially, the Games were relatively modest in scope. As time went by, however, they became increasingly elaborate and expensive, placing a heavy burden on host countries and cities and causing them to seek new means by which to raise the needed revenues. Television and radio rights have proven to be one lucrative source of such funds. So has the sale of marketing rights to large corporations, which flaunt the Olympic symbol and proclaim themselves to be "proud sponsors" of the Games. And so, in recent decades, has the sale of collector coins which issuers declare to be official Olympic issues.

The United States hosted a number of Olympics, both Summer and Winter, in the first 84 years of the modern Games. But the first U.S. Olympic coins didn't appear on the scene until 1984, when three special coins authorized by Congress marked and helped finance the Los Angeles Summer Games. Since then, the U.S. Mint has issued such coins routinely for every new Summer Olympiad — even when the Games took place on foreign soil. Typically, their issue price includes a hefty surcharge earmarked for Olympic-related programs. You could pay hundreds — or even thousands — of dollars to get complete sets of these coins. But given their high mintages and high issue prices, your only reward is likely to be the inner glow of being a proud Olympic sponsor — and subsidizer.

Photo courtesy of Bowers and Merena.

W I N N E R   N O .   1 5

An Isabella quarter graded Mint State-65

The United States Mint was 100 years old before it began producing commemorative coinage as most collectors understand that term — coinage that is issued to honor a particular person, place or event and sold at a premium to help raise funds for a worthy cause. The event that brought the first such coins into being was the World's Columbian Exposition, a world's fair held in Chicago to commemorate the 400th anniversary of Christopher Columbus' voyages of discovery to America.

The Columbian Exposition was a highly ambitious venture involving the creation of a virtual new city along the shore of Lake Michigan, complete with 160 buildings and 65,000 exhibits showcasing Americans' impressive advances in architecture, art, science, technology and other fields of human endeavor. The project ended up costing some $30 million — more than $1 for each of the 28 million visitors it attracted. That may sound piddling today, but at that time a dollar constituted much of a day's pay for many Americans. To help defray these costs, the managers of the fair requested — and received — congressional authorization for special U.S. coins they could sell as souvenirs to raise funds.

Initially, Congress authorized just one coin: a half dollar bearing the likeness of Columbus. Some 2.5 million examples of this "Columbian half dollar" were minted in 1892 and again in 1893, and today they are considered quite common. A few months later, however, the exposition's Board of Lady Managers sought a separate coin reflecting women's role in the fair and in society as a whole. Congress responded by authorizing a 25-cent piece bearing the image of Spain's Queen Isabella, who, with her husband Ferdinand, financed Columbus' expeditions. Just 40,000 examples of this "Isabella quarter" were minted, and more than 25,000 later were melted. Today, it is a scarce and coveted coin — and while an example graded MS-65 will cost you more than $2,000, it is highly desirable, with excellent upside potential.

L O S E R   N O .   1 5

Proof American Eagles

Precious-metal coins can be valuable on two different levels. At a minimum, they are worth the value of the metal they contain. Beyond that, they can bring an additional premium — potentially a large one — based upon their value as collectibles. Common-date gold and silver coins in average circulated condition are priced on the basis of how much gold or silver they contain. Scarcer gold and silver coins generally are priced according to their numismatic — or collector — value, with intrinsic worth (their value as precious metal) providing a floor.

In recent years, some government mints have issued what are known as "bullion coins." These are official coins with legal-tender value — but unlike regular coins intended for circulation, these are meant primarily to serve as stores of value for their purchasers; they are designed to be saved, rather than spent. Among the more familiar gold bullion coins are South Africa's Krugerrand, Canada's Maple Leaf and Great Britain's Britannia. In 1986, the United States entered the bullion-coin market with a series of gold and silver coins known as "American Eagles." Dealers sell these to the public at a modest premium over their value as metal — a markup that covers the costs of production, distribution and marketing. And their price goes up or down in direct proportion to rises and falls in the value of precious metal.

In addition to the standard American Eagles, which might be likened to business-strike coins, the Mint also offers special proof examples every year. These carry issue prices well above their value as precious metal and far above face value (which is just a small fraction of bullion value). These coins are represented as collectibles because of their sharp detail, mirror surfaces and relatively low mintages. In reality, however, they are dolled-up bullion coins — and while they may be beautiful to behold, they're unlikely to bring you a handsome return.

Photo courtesy of Bowers and Merena.

WINNER NO. 16

One-year type coins

Years ago, most collectors put together sets of U.S. coins according to date and mint mark. They would seek to acquire one Buffalo nickel, for example, for every date in the series and every mint that issued the coin that year. Thus, they would save three Buffalo nickels dated 1936 and three dated 1937, since production took place during those two years at three different mints — Philadelphia, Denver and San Francisco. Folders and albums sold to house sets of coins provided slots for every different "date-and-mint" combination.

In recent years, many collectors have abandoned date-and-mint collecting and turned instead to assembling sets of "type coins." Rather than encompassing every date in a series from every different mint, a "type set" contains just one example of any particular coin, or one example of every major type within that series. A type set, then, might include only one Buffalo nickel — probably a high-grade specimen of a common-date issue. At most, it might include two Buffalo nickels — one with the bison on a mound, the other with the revised reverse where the mound gives way to a plain, flattened surface.

Photo courtesy of Capital Pastics

Major types are often one-year issues. Frequently, problems arise when a coin is first produced and the Mint makes adjustments to fix them before the next year's run. That's what happened in 1913, when the first Buffalo nickels proved too prone to wear on the raised mound. The problem was corrected even before that year's production ended. Since demand is high for these one-year type coins and the supply is limited to just that single year, there's strong upward pressure on their value. Some are relatively common; the Variety 1 Buffalo nickel isn't a scarce issue, for example. Others are quite rare: These include the 1793 Chain cent and the 1796 Draped Bust quarter. All, however, benefit from being one-year type coins. Everything else being equal, this is a big advantage and you should view it as such.

LOSER NO. 16

Coins offered for sale on home-shopping television programs

Cable television has brought many changes to Americans' lifestyle, giving them programming options they never had before. One of those options is the chance to see merchandise up close and personal (and from every conceivable angle), hear it described in loving detail by rapturous (and some would say raptor-ous) shills — and then buy one or more of everything in sight simply by calling the 800 number on the screen. I'm speaking, of course, about the various home-shopping programs — and full-fledged shopping networks — that have sprung up like weeds in recent years.

Many find these programs entertaining. Some insist they've picked up great bargains by watching these shows. Perhaps they have, but based on what I've seen, those bargains haven't included collectible coins. The segments I have viewed, and the merchandise I have been shown by consumers who acquired it through these shows, leave little doubt in my mind that this is among the very worst ways to purchase coins.

By their very nature, these programs don't lend themselves to selling collector coins that are truly rare. They depend upon high-volume sales, so they have to deal in products that exist in substantial quantities. Thus, right off the bat, the coins they offer for sale are less-than-prime collectibles. Beyond that, this format is expensive for the sellers; they have to turn a profit not only for themselves but also for the people providing them with air time — and television air time isn't cheap. You, the consumer, end up subsidizing both these profit margins by paying excessive prices for the merchandise. These coins are often packaged very cleverly — put together in sets that stress their romantic background and their role in our nation's history. Look beyond the sizzle, though, and you will soon discover that the steak is low-grade and high-priced.

Photo courtesy of Bowers and Merena.

WINNER NO. 17

Better-date silver dollars

The year 2000 is just around the corner as this is written, and it will clearly be a milestone for mankind. Few flips of the calendar involve a change in all four digits in the date. Life will change in many ways, both obvious and subtle, as the new millennium begins, and one of those changes will be the appearance of a new dollar coin in Americans' pocket change. It will be smaller than traditional silver dollars from the nation's frontier days; instead, it will be the size of the Susan B. Anthony dollar — though with crucial modifications (such as special golden color) to avoid the major problems that dogged that ill-fated coin. But the new coin seems certain to focus new attention on the full-size cartwheels of the past.

Even without a burst of new publicity, silver dollars are hardly shrinking violets. Over the last quarter-century, they have been perennial pace-setters in the coin market — with the Morgan dollar, especially, reigning as king of the hill. There are good reasons for this. These are large, bulky coins with high precious-metal content — more than three-quarters of an ounce of silver; they're old, often dating back more than a hundred years; and many are extremely well preserved, since millions never left bank and government vaults.

Photo courtesy of Bowers and Merena.

These qualities give silver dollars exceptional appeal not only to collectors but also to investors purchashing coins for their portfolios.

Many Morgan dollars and other traditional cartwheels have bright, dazzling luster and razor-sharp detail. You need to be careful, however, not to fall in love with just a pretty face. Certain common-date dollars — the 1880-S and 1881-S, for example — exist in large quantities in pristine mint condition and really aren't worth what many dealers charge for them. You should concentrate instead on coins with lower mintages, even though their condition might be a bit less spectacular. They needn't be rare, only scarce. The 1886-S Morgan dollar and 1928 Peace dollar are two good examples. These coins will always be in demand, yet they're difficult to promote because they don't exist in tremendous numbers. They're safer and sounder values.

L O S E R   N O .   1 7

Mint State-67 commemorative coins priced far above the Mint State-66 level

Unlike regular-issue coins (the kind minted for use in everyday commerce), most commemorative coins are not produced primarily to be spent. Rather, they are meant as souvenirs, fund-raisers, mementos and forms of national tribute. They are special coins struck for special occasions, and frequently this status is underscored by the use of fancy packaging to house them when they are issued. Uncle Sam nets a profit from selling these coins, and so do organizations designated by Congress to benefit from the proceeds. The U.S. Olympic Committee, for example, has been on the receiving end several times.

The packaging and marketing were less sophisticated during the so-called "traditional" era of U.S. commemorative coinage, which extended from 1892 to 1954. Still, many of the commemoratives issued during that period did reach initial purchasers in holders which, at least, provided basic protection from wear and mishandling. Thus, when these coins were set aside in drawers or boxes or whatever, they stood a good chance of surviving in a high state of preservation — unlike regular coins, which typically lack such protection.

It stands to reason that a coin graded Mint State-67 will command a higher premium than a similar coin graded Mint State-66. It's also understandable that in some instances, that premium may be quite substantial. Coins in certain series — and certain dates within a given series — become extremely scarce when you reach that rarified level of preservation. But different ground rules apply with commemorative coins. With them, the survival rate is considerably higher in upper mint-state levels. Therefore, the extra premium shouldn't be as great. There are exceptions, to be sure, but as a general rule, you should be wary when the price gap between these two grade levels is dramatic.

Photo courtesy of Bowers and Merena.

WINNER NO. 18

The 1915 Panama-Pacific $50 gold piece, either octagonal or round

The Panama Canal is truly a wonder of the modern world — a manmade work every bit as stupendous in its way as the pyramids of Egypt and the rest of the seven wonders of ancient times. The notion of constructing a canal across the narrow isthmus of Panama had been conceived as early as the 16th century, when Spanish conquistadors first arrived in the region. Even then, its strategic value as a navigation shortcut was apparent. France made the first attempt to build such a canal in 1880, but was forced to abandon the effort ten years later. Congress authorized a U.S. venture in 1902 and work got under way the following year. After overcoming formidable engineering and medical obstacles, American canal-builders finished the massive project a decade later and the waterway opened to traffic in 1914.

Americans were justifiably proud of this achievement, and to celebrate the feat, a national party was scheduled in San Francisco in 1915. Actually, the party was global in nature: It was billed as the Panama-Pacific International Exposition and was meant as a kind of grand-scale house warming — or canal warming — officially marking the opening of this wonderful new resource that would, after all, improve the lot of humanity as a whole. To mark the festive occasion and help finance its costs, Congress also authorized five special coins for sale to the show's visitors (and others who might want them) at a premium.

The "Pan-Pac" coins included a silver half dollar, a gold dollar, a quarter eagle (or $2.50 gold piece) and two $50 gold pieces — the first U.S. coins ever issued in that denomination. The $50 coins were identical in design, both depicting the Greek goddess Minerva on the obverse and her symbol, the owl, on the reverse; one was round, however, while the other was octagonal. These coins have been acclaimed for their beauty. Even more attractive to investment-minded buyers are their mintages: After unsold specimens were melted, the net remaining figures were 685 octagonal pieces and 483 round. These coins are expensive, typically bringing strong five-figure prices. But they're rare, beautiful, desirable — and likely to rise in value as time goes by.

LOSER NO. 18

The 1986 Statue of Liberty $5 gold piece

Few, if any, symbols of American democracy are better known and better loved than the Statue of Liberty. This sentinel of freedom stands watch in New York Harbor, silently proclaiming Americans' bedrock belief in individual liberty and serving as a beacon for newly arriving immigrants seeking a share of that timeless dream. The statue was conceived by French historian Edouard de Laboulaye following the U.S. Civil War; he envisioned it as a way for the people of his country to show their admiration for Americans' lofty ideals. Sculptor Frederic Auguste Bartholdi devoted nearly two decades to the project. Upon the statue's completion in 1885, it stood 151 feet, 1 inch high and weighed 225 tons. It was disassembled and shipped to New York City, where it was dedicated on October 28, 1886, by President Grover Cleveland.

U.S. commemorative coinage had resumed in 1982 after a hiatus of nearly three decades — and as the time approached for the Statue of Liberty's 100th anniversary, sentiment arose to issue special coins for the occasion. Besides being tributes to this powerful national symbol, the coins could be sold at a premium to help raise funds for needed restoration of the statue and nearby Ellis Island, site of the reception center where many thousands of immigrants had been processed in bygone years as a first step on the road to becoming citizens. Congress authorized three such coins: a copper-nickel half dollar, a silver dollar and a $5 gold piece (or half eagle).

Production limit for the half eagle was set at 500,000 — not low, by any means, but relatively modest for a coin with such a popular theme. When orders exceeded that limit, a buying frenzy developed, driving up the price well beyond the level at which the coin was issued. But later, as demand receded, so, too, did the price — and as this is written, the coin is being offered for slightly less than what the Mint charged originally ($160 uncirculated and $170 proof). Given the ample supply, I see little likelihood this coin will enjoy much price appreciation in the future.

Photo courtesy of Bowers and Merena.

WINNER NO. 19

The 1864-L Indian Head cent in Extremely Fine condition or better

The Indian Head cent has long been a special favorite with collectors, and in its day it was viewed with great affection by Americans as a whole. Like the Buffalo nickel, it evokes a bygone era when the nation hadn't yet reached full maturity and life was simpler and sweeter — in short, the "good old days." Relations between white settlers and Native American tribes were tumultuous, even down-right hostile, during much of the period when this coin was being produced, from 1859 to 1909, but its portrait of an Indian clad in a feather headdress has come to serve as a symbol of our heritage and a tribute to the role that Native Americans played in that panorama.

A quaint, endearing story has persisted through the years that the Indian cent's designer, James Barton Longacre, used his daughter Sarah as his model in preparing the portrait. Supposedly, he sketched it while the young girl posed in a war-bonnet replica. This story gained credence from the fact that the "Indian's" features seem more like those of a white man. It now seems unlikely that such a scenario happened; sketches of similar portraits have turned up in Longacre's notebooks from much earlier, indicating a more generic source for his inspiration. But in 1864, five years after the coin's introduction, the artist — then U.S. Mint chief engraver — did add a personal touch to the Indian cent: He engraved his initial "L" on the war bonnet's ribbon.

The "L" appears only on bronze Indian cents; copper-nickel specimens from the series' earliest years don't have the designer's initial. And not all bronze cents dated 1864 have the letter, since Longacre didn't add it till late in the year. In fact, collectors have found that 1864 cents with "L" on the ribbon are quite scarce. This has made the coin a coveted collectible, worth hundreds or even thousands of dollars in top condition. Because it is inconspicuous and wears off quickly in circulation, the "L" is readily visible only on coins in at least high circulated grades. The 1864-L Indian Head cent is a legitimate, time-tested rarity with excellent upside potential.

L O S E R   N O .   1 9

Modern proof coins in very high grades at ridiculously high prices

Proofs are special coins in more ways than one. Mint technicians choose the very finest planchets (or coin blanks) for proofs — highly polished blanks totally free from blemish. They then strike these blanks multiple times with dies that are likewise highly polished. And rather than being tossed in a bin with other newly struck coins, each proof is handled individually and carefully by skilled work-men wearing rubber gloves. All this loving care results in coins with razor-sharp detail, flawless surfaces and, in many cases, breathtaking cameo contrast between the mirror-like fields (or background areas) and the frosted devices (or raised portions bearing the design and the inscriptions).

There isn't any question that proof coins are the ultimate,

when viewed from the standpoint of quality. They're head and shoulders above their business-strike cousins — the coins that are produced for use in everyday commerce. And in modern times, particularly since 1968, proofs from the U.S. Mint have been housed in elaborate packaging that shields them quite effectively from mishandling or other damage. Thus, they not only come in pristine condition to begin with, but remain in that exceptional level of preservation far longer than the proofs of previous eras.

It's perfectly understandable that coins with such pizzazz would command a premium. All the extra effort, all the loving care, all the special handling and all the fancy packaging — these come at a cost and the Mint is fully justified in passing it along. On the other hand, modern proofs — for all their positive features — do have one serious drawback when compared with the proofs of the past: Their quantity, like their quality, is quite high. And unlike high quality, large quantity is a depressant on market value. What's more, their protective packaging keeps these coins in extremely high condition — so even in grades of Proof-67 and above, they're relatively common. Some unscrupulous dealers price them as if they were scarce, but they are decidedly not and you should run, not walk, from any shop where that's the case.

Photo courtesy of Bowers and Merena.

WINNER NO. 20

The 1793 Chain and Wreath cents

E arly American coppers — the large cents and half cents minted by Uncle Sam in our nation's formative years — enjoy a devoted following in the coin collecting hobby. These pure copper coins represent a link with the earliest days of our nation and the fledgling U.S. Mint, and possess a simple charm that transforms mere collecting into a lifelong love affair for many of those who pursue them. This passion is intensified by the fact that early coppers come in seemingly endless varieties, with overdates, small dates, large dates, tall dates and various permutations of lettering, portraiture and other design elements keeping collectors constantly on their toes.

The very first U.S. cents, from the long-ago year of 1793, are among the most intriguing of them all. The Mint launched production in its modest Philadelphia home by issuing a coin that came to be known as the "Chain cent." The obverse of this coin bears a right-facing female head meant to signify Liberty, while the reverse shows the words ONE CENT within a chain of interlocking links. To the Mint's surprise and dismay, the coin encountered hostility from the outset. "The chain on the reverse is but a bad omen for liberty," sniffed one journalist, "and liberty herself appears to be in a fright." People saw the chain not as a symbol of unity, as the Mint intended, but as a suggestion of slavery. The design was quickly replaced by a new one with a modified portrait of Liberty and a wreath on the reverse in place of the chain. Before the year was over, the Wreath cent was gone as well, giving way to a Liberty Cap design.

The Chain cent and Wreath cent are obviously coins of tremendous historical significance. More than that, however, both are major rarities. The Mint produced only about 36,000 Chain cents and 63,000 Wreath cents, and in both cases those mintages are subdivided into several highly collectible varieties. You can expect to pay hundreds of dollars for low-grade specimens of either coin and thousands for high-grade examples, but they're worth it. Seldom in U.S. coinage have history, rarity and romance intersected so dramatically — and so appealingly.

LOSER NO. 20

Bags of uncirculated late-date coins

During the early 1960s, the hottest things on the market were uncirculated rolls of modern U.S. coins — Lincoln cents, Jefferson nickels, Roosevelt dimes and other contemporary series. The thinking was that if one bright new coin was worth collecting, a whole roll was fifty times — or forty times, or twenty times — more desirable and potentially more profitable in the long run. Few stopped to ponder that coins available by the roll probably weren't worth a whole lot to begin with, or that ultimately, the fifty coins in a roll would have to find their way into fifty different collections in order for their value to be maximized.

Roll collecting fizzled in the mid-1960s when market prices plunged, and nowadays the emphasis is on individual coins in top condition. Some dealers still offer rolls, though, and some collectors — or accumulators — still buy them up and put them away, figuring that their day is bound to come. Carrying this approach to an even greater (and even less logical) extreme, some buy and sell by the bag. In the case of Lincoln cents, there are 5,000 coins — with a total face value of $50 — in each bag, and a price exceeding $100 per bag is not uncommon for uncirculated coins.

Buying bags of coins isn't necessarily a terrible idea. In 1995, for example, some aggressive hobbyists purchased bags of that year's cents in hopes of finding examples of the '95 doubled-die variety — a coin that was then bringing a premium of more than $100. Some struck it rich — in a modest way, at least — by doing just that. Buying bags of silver coins may produce a profit if silver rises in value (assuming that the bags are purchased at minimal markup over their silver value to begin with). But as a general rule, bags should not be bought with an eye to profit potential, especially if that profit is tied to their value as collectibles. True collectors put together sets one coin at a time — not fifty, and certainly not 5,000. And without true collectors to give these coins a home, their profit potential is minimal.

Photo courtesy of Bowers and Merena.

WINNER NO. 21

The Gobrecht dollar

Although the dollar is the fundamental unit of the U.S. monetary system, there have been long stretches when no dollar coins were produced by the U.S. Mint. One such stretch occurred in the early 19th century. After completing production of 1803 silver dollars in the early part of 1804, the Mint suspended output of this denomination, leaving it on the sidelines for thirty years. Researchers now believe that the rare silver dollars dated 1804 actually came into being in 1834, when the State Department had them struck as gifts for Asian monarchs — choosing the earlier date because it was the last calendar year in which dollar coins had been issued.

The 1804 dollars have a fascinating story all their own. However, they were not the only new dollar coins minted by Uncle Sam in the 1830s. Not long after the diplomatic episode that gave rise to those backdated coins, the Mint began work on an altogether different silver dollar — one with a fresh and dramatic new design. The job of preparing this coin was assigned to Christian Gobrecht, a gifted engraver and medalist who joined the Mint staff in 1835 and later would become its chief engraver. Gobrecht was given designs by two talented artists, Thomas Sully and Titian Peale, and told to use them as the basis for a pair of coinage dies. The stunningly beautiful coin that resulted is known as the Gobrecht dollar.

The Mint struck a series of Gobrecht dollars from 1836 to 1839 — some as patterns, others for use in commerce and all in extremely small numbers. Essentially, these were transitional coins leading up to the start of the Liberty Seated series. In fact, the Gobrecht dollar introduced the Liberty Seated obverse to U.S. coinage. The eagle on its reverse was a bird of a different feather, though, and many critics consider it far superior to the one that perched on Seated coinage of varied denominations for half a century. Gobrecht dollars are rare, beautiful and distinctive — and if you can afford the typical five-figure price tag, these are great coins to own.

LOSER NO. 21

A complete run of late-date proof sets from 1968 to date

At one time, in the 1950s and early 1960s, collectors looked upon newly issued proof sets as a lead-pipe cinch to appreciate in value — and their confidence was justified. During that period, the U.S. Mint offered these sets for $2.10 apiece, and by the time purchasers got their sets from the government in the mail, they inevitably were worth more — sometimes quite a bit more. Many collectors — and non-collectors, too — ordered sets in quantities of ten, twenty, fifty or even more, sold off the extras within a short time and pocketed the profit. Some put them away as a hedge against inflation or a nest egg for retirement, or to pay for their children's education.

All this changed in 1968, when the Mint reintroduced proof sets after a three-year lapse caused by a coin shortage during the mid-1960s. The dime and quarter no longer contained precious metal, and the half dollar's silver content was down from 90 percent to only 40. Worse yet, the issue price was more than twice as high; the Mint had raised it from $2.10 per set to $5. In effect, Uncle Sam skimmed off the "guaranteed" profit for himself. Instead of being surefire winners, proof sets became a crapshoot for people who procured them from the Mint. Since that time, in fact, they have been a losing proposition on the whole — thanks, in large part, to numerous price increases that have boosted the issue price to $12.50 per set as this is written. Anyone who has purchased every single proof set at issue price from the Mint from 1968 to the present is using red ink in his or her ledger book (unless he or she was fortunate enough to get one or more of the very few sets containing mint errors).

Doesn't this suggest that a full run of proof sets dating back to 1968 would be a bargain today? After all, many are selling now for less than issue price. In a word, the answer is no. The supply of late-date proof sets far exceeds the demand — so unless and until a lot more collectors are created for this material, it's likely to languish for years to come. The many hundreds of dollars it would cost you for these sets can be spent much more wisely on truly scarce coins.

Photo courtesy of Bowers and Merena.

WINNER NO. 22

The 1912-S Liberty Head nickel

The 1913 Liberty Head nickel has one of the highest profiles — and one of the highest values — of any U.S. coin. Only five examples are known, and in 1996 one of them changed hands for close to $1.5 million at the sale of the famous collection of Louis E. Eliasberg Sr. In doing so, it became the first U.S. coin ever to exceed the million-dollar mark at public auction. As even novice collectors are well aware, however, 1913 Liberty nickels weren't issued officially by the U.S. Mint. In fact, it is believed that all five known examples were struck surreptitiously — and illegally — by a larcenous employee at the Philadelphia Mint who kept them under wraps until he could no longer be punished for this crime by the federal government.

A far less famous, far less valuable — but far more legitimate — rarity occurred in the same nickel series just one year earlier. It will never be a million-dollar coin, but in top mint condition it's worth several thousand dollars. And unlike its 1913 cousin, it's a genuine Mint issue that actually was produced for circulation. The coin in question is the 1912-S Liberty nickel — the first U.S. coin of this denomination ever to be struck at the San Francisco Mint.

From 1883 — when the Liberty nickel first appeared —

Photo courtesy of Bowers and Merena.

through 1911, every coin in this series was minted in Philadelphia. Not until 1912, the final year of the series (at least from the government's perspective), did branch mints get a piece of the action. The Denver Mint produced nearly 8.5 million examples that year, while San Francisco issued just 238,000. Disregarding the 1913, that's easily the lowest mintage in the series — the only one, in fact, below a million. The '12-S nickel costs upwards of $100 even in grades as low as Very Fine. It's a coin worth owning in any condition, however, because of its low mintage and its high collector base.

L O S E R   N O .   2 2

The 1883 Liberty Head nickel without the word CENTS graded Mint State-65

The Liberty Head nickel is one of the simplest, most straightforward coins ever issued by Uncle Sam. Its design is broad and open, with little subtlety, and its minimal inscriptions are neatly arranged and inconspicuous. The series itself was similarly uncomplicated, for the most part, with hardly any varieties to speak of and branch-mint issues appearing in just one year, 1912, the last official year before this coin gave way to the Buffalo nickel. There was plenty of intrigue at the end of the series, though, with the unofficial striking of the rare 1913 specimens — and also lots of excitement at the beginning.

In designing the Liberty nickel, the U.S. Mint's chief engraver, Charles E. Barber, placed a large letter "V" — the Roman numeral representing "5" — on the reverse, within a simple wreath. This paralleled the design of the then-current nickel three-cent piece, where the Roman numeral III was on the reverse. Barber saw no need to add the word CENTS; after all, it didn't appear on the three-cent piece. Soon after the nickel first hit circulation, though, crafty con men began to gold-plate it and pass it off on unsuspecting merchants as a new $5 gold piece. They were aided in this chicanery by the absence of that crucial word CENTS. Barber hastily prepared a new reverse design incorporating that word, and this — plus word of mouth — resolved the problem.

Production of Liberty nickels in 1883 included both varieties; by year's end, the Mint had struck a total of about 21.5 million of the new nickels, and nearly three-fourths of them — more than 16 million — had the word CENTS on the reverse. Mintage of the no-CENTS variety, having been halted early in the year, totaled less than 5.5 million. But people set aside the earlier variety in substantially greater numbers than the later one, reasoning that because it had been replaced, it would bring a handsome premium down the line. In fact, just the opposite has occurred: The second variety, with the word CENTS, is much scarcer today in pristine mint condition because it wasn't saved to nearly the same extent. The no-CENTS nickel, on the other hand, is the lowest-priced coin in the entire series in MS-65, currently bringing about $325 in that grade. Even at that, I would avoid it. Just too many mint-fresh examples were saved, and too many still exist.

Photo courtesy of Bowers and Merena.

WINNER NO. 23

The 1937-D three-legged Buffalo nickel

F reak accidents can cause major financial hardship —
not to mention injury or death — when they happen
on the highway. They can lead to a bonanza, though,
when they happen in the press room at one of the U.S.
mints. Consider the case of the "three-legged" Buffalo nickel. This fascinating mint-error coin, now a popular variety
worth hundreds — even thousands — of dollars, came into
being because a Mint workman failed to clean up properly
after such an accident.

A coin is produced when a planchet (or coin blank) is
stamped simultaneously by two dies — one imparting the
obverse design, the other the reverse. Occasionally, the
machinery jams and fails to feed a planchet into position.
When that happens, the dies strike each other instead and
each incurs damage from the other. These damaged dies are
said to have "clash marks," and standard procedure calls for
stopping the press and removing them from service. But on
one such occasion in 1937, a workman at the Denver Mint
decided to take a shortcut: Instead of replacing the dies, he
pulled out an emery stick and ground off the clash marks on
a Buffalo nickel die. He may not have noticed it at first, but
this removed not only the unwanted marks but also much of

the foreleg of the bison on the die for the coin's reverse. Significant numbers of nickels were struck with this defect and escaped into circulation before the problem was spotted and corrected.

No one knows for sure exactly how many "three-legged" 1937-D nickels got out. The figure is believed to be relatively modest, however. And over the years, this "accidental" coin has caught collectors' fancy and become a widely recognized and much desired part of the Buffalo series. It will cost you more than $100 even in the lowly grade of good, and more than $1,000 in mint condition. The cost is justified, though, for while this coin may be a freak, it's legitimately scarce and perennially popular with a broad range of collectors.

LOSER NO. 23

Mint-error coins where significant magnification is needed to see the mistake

Mint errors have become increasingly popular with collectors in recent years. Major mistakes have always enjoyed a following and always commanded a premium. The three-legged Buffalo nickel attests to this; so do such overdate coins as the 1918-over-17-D Buffalo nickel, the 1918-over-17-S Standing Liberty quarter and the 1942-over-41 Mercury dime. All of these are viewed not only as important varieties but also as desirable — and valuable — rarities. But over the last three decades or so, error-coin collecting has expanded from a fascinating specialty with a relatively modest but enthusiastic following into one of the biggest growth areas in the hobby. And its devotees are looking for ever-less conspicuous minting mistakes.

Part of the explanation undoubtedly lies in the fact that scarce-date coins, precious-metal issues and other coins with premium value are so much harder to find today in ordinary pocket change. A generation ago, collectors could go to the bank, pick up a few dozen rolls of cents, nickels or other current coins, take them home, examine them, and turn up quite a few that were worth at least a modest amount above face. Today, they have to look harder and closer to find collectible coins: Instead of seeking coins with scarce dates or valuable date-and-mint combinations, they look for coins with interesting and potentially scarce imperfections. This kind of searching paid off in 1995, when sharp-eyed collectors found noticeable doubling on some of that year's cents from the Philadelphia Mint. Those coins turned out to be more common than first believed, but they still bring a decent premium.

To mint-error specialists, even small mistakes can be highly appealing. You should be wary, however, of paying a big premium for a mint error so small that it needs to be examined under a magnifying glass in order to be seen and appreciated. Size does count in this instance. As a general rule, the bigger and more obvious the mistake, the greater the premium value.

Photo courtesy of Bowers and Merena.

WINNER NO. 24

The two-cent piece in Mint State-65 Red

The two-cent piece was one of the shortest-lived coins in U.S. history, lasting barely ten years before it was consigned to the burial ground for dead denominations. It left an enduring legacy, though, for while it failed to carve a niche for itself in circulation, it will always be remembered as the coin that introduced the now-familiar motto IN GOD WE TRUST.

This large bronze coin was very much a product of its times — and specifically a result of the Civil War. Two separate war-related influences combined to bring it about. One was the almost total disappearance of existing U.S. coinage during the first few years of that epic conflict: Hoarding became a national obsession, with gold and silver coins vanishing from circulation first, followed soon afterward by copper and copper-nickel issues. Observing the wide acceptance of privately issued small bronze tokens as emergency wartime money, the Treasury decided in 1864 to slenderize the Indian Head cent and change its composition from copper-nickel to bronze. At the same time, it introduced a larger bronze companion, the two-cent piece, to help reinforce the beachhead it was seeking to establish for new coins in circulation. Meanwhile, religious fervor —

Photo courtesy of Bowers and Merena.

kindled by the agonies of the war — gave rise to sentiment for recognizing God on the nation's coinage, and the two-cent piece was chosen to serve as a showcase for that tribute.

Initially, two-cent pieces circulated widely, filling the coinage void as they were intended to do. Within a few years, though, the public began to shun them as older coins reappeared and newer, more convenient alternatives were produced in the postwar years. Mintage shrunk from nearly 20 million in 1864 to only 65,000 in 1872. Only proofs were issued in 1873, and after that the series was laid to rest. Because of the high usage of early two-cent pieces and the low mintage of later ones, relatively few exist today in pristine mint condition. Even among the ones that were saved initially, many were mishandled over the years. In Mint State-65, common-date examples cost $400 or more today — but the price is right, for these are truly scarce, historic coins.

LOSER NO. 24

Proof coins priced excessively high because their business-strike counterparts are scarce

We've all heard the expression that you can't compare apples and oranges. Yet, now and then, people who buy and sell coins do just that. They do it when they assign an inordinately high value to a proof coin just because the regular-quality coin of the same type and date — the business-strike version — is scarce and commands a premium above the market value of common-date issues. The business strike here is the apple and the proof is the orange — and just because the apple is exceptionally tasty and desirable, that doesn't make the orange any juicier.

Consider the case of the 1877 Indian Head cent. This has long been regarded as the single biggest "key" in the Indian series. It's one of only two Indian cents with mintages below a million — and while the other coin (the 1909-S) was made in smaller numbers, the 1877 is worth more across the board, in every single grade, because it was saved in far smaller quantities and distributed much more widely. But what we're referring to here is the "apple" factor — the business-strike mintage of the coin. At 852,500, it's exceptionally scarce by the standards of cent collecting, and the high ongoing demand justifies the premium this coin has always brought. The U.S. Mint also produced about 900 proof cents in 1877 — but while that is surely a modest figure, it's higher than the proof mintages of the 1874 and 1875 Indian cents, both of which were struck in quantities of only about 700. Yet the 1877 is valued at four times as much in Proof-65 — $2,000, compared with $500 for each of the other two dates.

Clearly, this is a case where the value of the apple has inflated the price tag of the orange. There is no evidence that proof 1877 cents have suffered a higher attrition rate than the two earlier proofs. If anything, those should be worth more since they have lower mintages. In short, proofs should be compared with proofs, regardless of the corresponding business-strike mintages. Some spillover effect is inevitable — but a fourfold higher premium is excessive.

Photo courtesy of Bowers and Merena.

WINNER NO. 25

Shield nickels graded Proof-65 or higher

In recent years, Americans have gotten by with only four truly circulating coins — the cent, nickel, dime and quarter. The U.S. Mint produces half dollars for circulation, but they see little actual use. Starting in 2000, a dollar coin also will be struck for use in daily commerce, but as of this writing it's anyone's guess how widely it will circulate. Conditions were far different in the 19th century, when the Mint routinely made upwards of a dozen different coins for circulation — sometimes including two different kinds with the same face value.

Five-cent pieces furnished one example of duplication. Right from the start of U.S. federal coinage in the early 1790s, the Mint had produced a small silver coin called the half dime, which, as its name suggests, weighed exactly half as much as the dime. In 1865, with gold and silver coins still among the missing because of Civil War hoarding, the Mint decided to strike a copper-nickel five-cent piece as a means to help retire the fractional five-cent notes issued by the government on an emergency basis during the war. The new coin made its debut in 1866 and came to be known as the Shield nickel because of the ornate shield shown on its obverse.

Photo courtesy of Bowers and Merena.

A case can be made that the Shield nickel was one of the ugliest coins in U.S. history. It certainly was one of the least aesthetic, with the uninspiring shield on one side and the simple number "5" on the reverse. Whatever its shortcomings, though, it did establish the copper-nickel five-cent piece, or "nickel," as a useful, popular coin. And over the years, it has gained favor itself with many collectors — not because of its appearance but because of the genuine scarcity of many dates in the series. Shield nickels were minted for 17 years, and in only three of those years did production exceed 10 million. Proofs were produced every year, and their mintages were generally very low — less than 1,000, in many cases. Even a "common-date" Proof-65 example will cost you close to $500, but at the market's high in 1989 that same coin would have cost $2,500. To me, it's a wonderful value at today's price and has tremendous potential.

LOSER NO. 25

Common-date Peace dollars graded Mint State-63 and 64

The Great War — only later renamed World War I — decimated the male populations of Britain, France, Germany and Austria-Hungary and also claimed the lives of more than 50,000 American "Doughboys." It was optimistically labeled "The War to End All Wars" — and after the declaration of an armistice on November 11, 1918, high-minded leaders and individual citizens the world over set out to ensure that such a conflagration would never happen again. To that end, they set up the League of Nations, hoping that a world body dedicated to peace would serve as a fire wall against any future war. Sadly, of course, the League — and that hope — would be in vain.

The League of Nations' failure stemmed in large measure from Uncle Sam's abandonment of the idealistic venture. Instead of joining the League, the United States retreated into a shell of isolationism, unwittingly helping thereby to sow the bitter seeds of an even more devastating conflict. The yearning for a lasting peace did give rise to tangible expressions of Americans' sentiment, though, and one of these took the form of a handsome new coin. The coin, a silver dollar, quickly came to be known as the "Peace dollar" because — alone among circulating U.S. coinage at this writing — it has the word PEACE as an inscription.

The Peace dollar had a short life span, from 1921 to 1935, and wasn't minted at all from 1929 through 1933, largely because of diminished need for coinage at the onset of the Great Depression. It tends to be weakly struck, and any imperfections are magnified by its broad, open design. As a consequence, it's quite scarce in the higher-end grades of Mint State-65 and above. At the same time, it exists in relatively high numbers in the mid-range grades of Mint State-63 and 64, especially in the case of common-date issues. A large supply translates into lower market value and serves as a depressant on future potential. That's a yellow warning light for you, the consumer: This is not the best road to go down.

WINNER NO. 26

Classic Head half cents graded Mint State-63 to 65, BN and RB

There's widespread clamor today to do away with the cent. Critics contend that it serves no useful purpose, needlessly taxes the U.S. Mint's production facilities and ends up simply cluttering people's pockets, purses and drawers. As Andy Rooney showed on TV's "60 Minutes," the coin has fallen to such low esteem that most people can't be bothered bending over to pick one up — or even to pick up several in a cluster. Given this state of affairs, it's hard to imagine a time when the cent wasn't even the lowest-value coin in U.S. commerce. Yet for more than sixty years, from the dawn of federal coinage in 1793 to the eve of the Civil War, Americans did indeed have such a coin: a pure copper "half cent" that was not only half the value of the cent, but more than twice the size of the current Lincoln "penny."

The fact that such a coin was issued in the first place underscores how low consumer prices were — by present-day standards, that is — in the formative years of our nation. At 6.74 grams, the earliest half cents were 20 percent heavier than today's Washington quarter; then again, their purchasing power was comparable to that of the current quarter. The size was reduced to 5.44 grams in 1800, and remained there through the half cent's last hurrah in 1857.

Production of half cents was modest and intermittent, exceeding a million in only two years and falling below 100,000 more than a dozen times — not even counting the entire decade of the 1840s, when only proofs were made. Today, every coin in the series brings upwards of $100 in mint condition — and, in some cases, in even the very lowest collectible grade. The Classic Head portion of the series, from

Photo courtesy of Bowers and Merena.

1809 to 1836, is especially appealing to many collectors and highly desirable in the grades of Mint State-63, 64 and 65. I recommend either brown (BN) or red-brown (RB) examples, since fully red (RD) pieces are susceptible to toning and loss of their substantial bonus premium. You'll pay anywhere from a couple of hundred dollars to several thousand, but you'll have a coin that's scarce, historic, beautiful and completely charming.

LOSER NO. 26

Picked-through rolls of uncirculated silver dollars

"**O**riginality counts." Those words are often heard in contests calling for entries of twenty-five words or less. Originality counts with collectible coins, as well: Dealers and collectors place a premium — often a high one — on coins with original luster, sets in original holders, or rolls that were assembled from the same original bag of mint-fresh coins. Being "original" translates into being free from tarnish, taint or tampering.

A generation ago, it was relatively easy to obtain an original roll — or, for that matter, a full original bag — of Morgan or Peace silver dollars. "Cartwheels" hadn't yet emerged as special favorites of investment-minded buyers; they were playing second fiddle to smaller, more modern coins in the marketplace of the early 1960s. A roll of common-date Morgans in BU (brilliant uncirculated) condition could be acquired then for about the same price as a single such coin today. And, more often than not, that roll would be original — just the way it came from an old-time bag, with all 20 coins matched closely in quality and appearance.

Over the years, the market changed dramatically. Modern coins lost favor; silver bullion rose in value sharply; and silver dollars came to be the darlings of a new breed of coin collector/investors. With this drastic change came heavy new emphasis on the quality of coins — their level of preservation. And that, in turn, led people with rolls and bags of coins, especially silver dollars, to scrutinize each coin and pull out any specimens with a little extra pizzazz — for even slight differences in luster, sharpness or toning could mean substantial difference in market value. This process was repeated time and again, to the point where truly original rolls are few and far between. You'll see BU dollar rolls advertised for sale, and the current bid price of $280 ($14 per coin) for common-date issues may seem attractive. Keep in mind, however, that you'll be getting sludge. The nice coins will be gone, and you'll be getting dregs no one else wanted.

Photo courtesy of Bowers and Merena.

WINNER NO. 27

Draped Bust silver dollars and half dollars graded AU-50 to AU-55

A dollar was big money in early America. Although the Founding Fathers established it as the cornerstone of the U.S. monetary system, it was too high an amount to be practical in the form of a single coin. As a result, silver dollars were minted sparingly, and in very small quantities, during the first decade or so of U.S. coinage — and not at all thereafter for more than 30 years. For all intents and purposes, the half dollar was the highest-value coin encountered in everyday commerce by most Americans.

Design changes were frequent in early U.S. coinage, and the silver dollar and half dollar both underwent several major revisions during the first few years of their existence. The very first coins of both denominations carried a "Flowing Hair" portrait of Miss Liberty, but this was soon discarded in favor of a more sedate — and decidedly more mature — likeness commonly referred to as the "Draped Bust" type. This made its debut on the dollar in 1795 and was placed on the half dollar the following year. It shows Miss Liberty facing to the right with a ribbon in her hair and drapery covering much, but not all, of her rather ample bosom. At first, the reverse of the Flowing Hair design, depicting a small eagle, was retained on the reverse, but later this gave way to an eagle with a shield upon its breast — an eagle that is said to be "heraldic."

The most famous Draped Bust dollar — the 1804 — is a story by itself and ranks among the most valuable of all U.S. coins. Few can hope to own this great rarity — but the earlier coins in the series, from 1795 to 1803, while attainable, also are far from inexpensive, for all have mintages under half a million and, in most cases, under 100,000. Draped Bust half dollars lingered until 1807, but topped 500,000 in just one year, 1806. Both denominations are prohibitively expensive in mint condition. They'll set you back several thousand dollars even in about uncirculated (AU) condition, but as rare, historic and highly coveted coins, they're well worth the outlay.

LOSER NO. 27

Russian 5-rouble gold coins certified in grades of Mint State-65 and above

Certification of rare coins by independent third-party grading services has been a boon to the market in recent years, greatly reducing contentiousness over coins' level of preservation and giving buyers and sellers a heightened sense of confidence. Certification of common coins has led to abuses, however, and one of the prime examples of this has been the extensive promotion and sale of Russian 5-rouble gold coins from the turn of the 20th century at highly inflated prices based upon the fact they've been certified in high mint-state grades.

The coins being offered are interesting from a historic standpoint: They carry the portrait of Nicholas II, last of the czars, who, along with the rest of the royal family, died at the hands of a firing squad following the Russian Revolution.

They also contain precious metal: not quite one-fifth of an ounce of gold, or slightly less than a U.S. half eagle ($5 gold piece). And as the grades assigned to them attest, they're in a high level of preservation. But the prices being charged by unscrupulous promoters are far above their actual market value.

To begin with, 5-rouble coins of Nicholas II were made in tremendous quantities. Some dates are scarce, to be sure, but others were produced in massive numbers: The 1898, for example, had a mintage of more than 52 million. And many pieces were saved in mint condition by the czar and later by Soviet authorities — stored in Swiss bank vaults very much the way that Morgan silver dollars remained in Treasury vaults in this country. As a result, these coins are readily available in mint condition — even in grades as high as Mint State-66 or 67. And whereas Morgan dollars are widely collected by date and coveted in high grades, most collectors acquire the Russian 5 roubles — if at all — as a type coin, and won't pay more than a nominal extra premium for high quality. As this is written, the 5-rouble coin contains less than $70 worth of gold at the current bullion value of $310 per ounce, yet some promoters are selling it for $1,200 in MS-67. To me, that's a rip-off. It's worth more than bullion, but closer to $120 than $1,200.

Photo courtesy of Bowers and Merena.

WINNER NO. 28

Early $2.50, $5 and $10 gold pieces in EF and AU condition

Gold has not been part of America's circulating coinage since 1933, and it saw little actual use in the nation's daily commerce even then. The Founding Fathers felt deeply, however, that issuing gold coins was important as a means to lend credibility and prestige to U.S. coinage — and to the nation itself — when the United States first took its place on the world stage, and the practice continued for nearly a century and a half. Not until the Great Depression ravaged the nation's economy did Uncle Sam retreat from this commitment.

The Mint Act of 1792 provided for the issuance of three gold coins: an eagle, or $10 gold piece; a half eagle ($5); and a quarter eagle ($2.50). The eagle and half eagle made their first appearances in 1795, with the quarter eagle joining them in 1796. Other denominations — most notably the double eagle (or $20 gold piece) — came along later, after the discovery of gold in California. But these three coins collectively formed the cornerstone of U.S. gold coinage, and they were the only ones produced before 1849.

When we refer to early U.S. gold coins, we really place the dividing line not in 1849, but rather a decade earlier. It was in 1838 that the U.S. Mint introduced the Coronet design on the gold coinage — and since this design persisted until 1908, it is usually associated with a more mature period of the Mint's history. During the early period, the eagle was produced only from 1795 to 1804 and came with a Capped Bust portrait of Miss Liberty. The half eagle was issued almost every year, but the quarter eagle appeared somewhat sporadically, and not at all from 1809 through 1820. Both went through a series of design changes, evolving from the early Capped Bust facing right to a different Capped Bust facing left, then to a Capped Head version and finally to the so-called Classic Head. All of these are charming, most have extremely low mintages and all are highly desirable. You'll pay thousands of dollars for one of these coins, even in EF or AU condition, but you'll have a solid collectible that's also an excellent investment. And at present, these coins are not much more expensive than they were in the 1970s.

LOSER NO. 28

Common-date British sovereigns in mint condition

The British sovereign is one of the best known and most historic gold coins in the world. First issued in 1489, it has remained in production for centuries, right into modern times, and has attained a high degree of recognition and use in many parts of the world. Its acceptance is so universal, in fact, that during World War II the survival kits issued to Allied fliers — intended for use if they were shot down in unfamiliar territory — included examples of this coin. Most sovereigns struck since 1817 have carried a portrait of St. George slaying a dragon, and this design — one of the most familiar in coinage history — has reinforced the coin's popularity and ready recognition.

Sovereigns have been produced not only by the British Royal Mint, but also by mints in far-flung outposts of the British Empire — and some of these are quite scarce and even rare. Many other sovereigns were struck by the millions, however, and are worth just a nominal premium over the market value of the metal they contain, which is slightly less than one-fourth of an ounce of gold. In effect, they are little more than bullion-type coins.

In recent years, fast-buck artists have found a way to reap big-league profits from these small-premium coins. They buy up common-date sovereigns in a high level of preservation — coins that are readily available in substantial quantities — and submit them to one of the third-party certification services. Then, when the coins are encapsulated with grades of, say, Mint State-65 or 66, they offer them for sale at greatly inflated prices as if they were rare and numismatically valuable in those grades. "There are tons of this stuff around," says respected hobby researcher R.W. Julian, "and it simply isn't worth a huge premium. A small premium, yes, but that's all." With gold bullion selling for $310 per ounce, a fair market price might be $100. If someone is charging much more, he or she is trying to rip you off.

Photo courtesy of Bowers and Merena.

WINNER NO. 29

Seated Liberty dollars graded AU-50 to AU-55

U.S. coin designs underwent frequent changes during the nation's formative years. The U.S. Mint seemed to be experimenting constantly — tinkering with the images it presented to the world through the medium of legal-tender coinage. Miss Liberty appeared with flowing hair, a Liberty Cap, a draped bust, a capped bust, a capped head, a Classic head, facing right, facing left — all in the first four decades of federal coinage. It was quite a contrast with the sameness of the nation's modern coinage, where design changes occur, if at all, at a glacial pace. Seemingly endless die varieties compounded the remarkable diversity.

By the mid–1830s, the nation had achieved a measure of maturity and stability, and it was time for U.S. coinage to do the same. Robert Maskell Patterson accelerated the process when he became Mint director in 1835. Patterson wanted to upgrade U.S. coin designs to put them on a par with those of Europe — and, with that in mind, he oversaw creation of a stunning new silver dollar by engraver Christian Gobrecht. This coin, first struck in 1836, served as the prototype for the Seated Liberty coinage, which remained in use thereafter for more than half a century.

Oddly, the dollar was the last silver coin to bear the permanent version of the Seated Liberty portraiture — the one that paired Miss Liberty with a heraldic eagle. The first silver dollar to carry this design didn't appear on the scene until 1840. And though it was produced on a regular annual basis until it was discontinued in 1873, mintages were modest — even minuscule — for the most part, exceeding 1 million (and doing so barely, at that) only in 1871 and 1872. Mintages below 100,000 — and even below 10,000 — were far more typical. As you might expect, these coins bring a pretty penny — thousands of dollars, in fact — in choice mint condition. High-grade circulated examples — certified as, say, About Uncirculated-50 or AU-55 — can be had for just a few hundred dollars, and while they may lack the sizzle of an MS-65 piece, they still give you plenty of "steak": scarce, historic coins in desirable, collectible condition.

LOSER NO. 29

Big-mintage modern commemorative coins from small, obscure countries

Of all the "losers" profiled in this book, there probably isn't a single one with more dismal investment potential than modern commemorative coins from obscure foreign countries — including some issuers that may not be countries at all. They range all the way from base-metal coins priced at less than $10 apiece to gold and platinum coins costing hundreds of dollars each, and possibly even thousands. But they have three things in common: issue prices far above the intrinsic worth of their metal, virtually no collector base, and absolutely zero upside potential to ever rise in value above what they'd bring as bullion.

Chances are you've seen commercials on TV, or ads in the paper, for coins from the Marshall Islands tied to some major event in the news or some noteworthy anniversary.

We saw this sort of thing when Britain's Princess Diana was killed, for example, and on the 25th anniversary of the Apollo 11 moon landing. The events certainly merited commemorative coinage, and a British coin scheduled for instance in 1999 to honor Princess Di will be a prime collectible. But Marshall Islands "coins" are really nothing but overpriced tokens and medals — and unlike British and U.S. coins, hardly anyone collects them. The only ones who profit are the Marshall Islands themselves and the people who are promoting this tawdry trash. Incidentally, did you know that two of the Marshall islands are Bikini and Eniwetok, where atomic bomb experiments took place after World War II? Now, this Pacific island chain is sending bombs to us!

While we're on the subject, you also should steer clear of the many new coins from the Isle of Man. These may have a bit more respectability than Marshall Islands issues, but they have about the same investment potential: the potential of a heat wave in Antarctica.

Photo courtesy of Bowers and Merena.

WINNER NO. 30

Copper-nickel Indian Head cents graded Mint State-64

The first small-size U.S. one-cent piece, the Flying Eagle cent, was popular with most Americans. By 1857, when this coin made its debut in circulation, people had grown tired of lugging around the pure copper "large cent" — for while they may not have referred to it by that term, its bulky size (not much smaller and lighter than our present-day half dollar) was weighing down, and wearing holes in, many of their pockets. But, while it was popular, the Flying Eagle cent had a fatal flaw: It was prone to weakness of strike because the high points on its obverse were opposite the high points on its reverse. The U.S. Mint's chief engraver, James B. Longacre, was directed to come up with a new design.

Longacre, who also designed the Flying Eagle cent, scored an even bigger hit with its replacement, for the coin he fashioned next — the Indian Head cent — went on to become one of this nation's most familiar and most admired. It remained in production for fully half a century before giving way to the even longer-running Lincoln cent in 1909.

Initially, the Indian cent had the same specifications as

the Flying Eagle. It was the same diameter as today's Lincoln cent but, at 4.67 grams, it weighed nearly twice as much. And it was struck from an alloy of 88-percent copper and 12-percent nickel, which gave it a light tan appearance and led some people to refer to it as a "white cent." After only two full years of production, however, it was caught up in the coin hoarding sparked by the Civil War and it virtually disappeared from circulation. In 1864, the Mint introduced a slenderized Indian cent made of bronze and thereby reestablished a beachhead in commerce for the coin. The copper-nickel version had been minted in only six years — 1859 through the first part of 1864. Although its annual mintages weren't small by the standards of the day, ranging between 10 million and 50 million, this "white" Indian cent enjoys wide popularity as a type coin. In Mint State-64, it costs about $150 (not counting the higher-priced 1859), but I consider that a good value.

LOSER NO. 30

"Double-trouble" coins

There's a certain amount of guesswork — and risk — involved in trying to figure out what kind of grade an uncertified (or "raw") coin will receive when it's submitted to one of the third-party grading services. The risk can be substantial, too, for small variations in the grade of a coin sometimes result in very large differences in that coin's market value. Further risk would seem to be eliminated once the coin is certified and encapsulated, for presumably it can be sold at that point for the value corresponding to the grade it has been assigned. But that's not necessarily true for all time and in each and every case. Experts can distinguish a "just-made-it" coin graded Mint State-65 from one that nearly qualifies for Mint State-66, for example, and they naturally have a preference — and perhaps a higher buying price — for premium-quality coins.

The risk is compounded — and so is the potential for erosion of your investment — when a coin has a special characteristic incorporated into its grade and, by extension, its market value. That's what happens with Morgan silver dollars that are classified as having Deep-Mirror Prooflike (DMPL) surfaces; or Mercury dimes with Full Split Bands on the fasces on the reverse; or Franklin half dollars with Full Bell Lines on the Liberty Bell. These qualities enhance the appeal and the value of these coins, but at the same time, they open a second front, so to speak, in the ongoing long-term battle over just what the coins are really worth.

I refer to these as "double-trouble" coins. The very characteristics that seem positive at the outset can have negative implications in the long run if a disagreement develops over the grading — as can and does happen even with certified coins — or if the coins at some point are removed from their grading-service holders. It's hard enough to get a consensus concerning the grade of a coin; it's doubly difficult to get complete agreement on a second point, such as whether the bell lines are really full. That gives people two things to disagree about, and that's double jeopardy.

Photo courtesy of Bowers and Merena.

WINNER NO. 31

Proof-65 Mercury dimes

The "Mercury" dime is widely acclaimed as one of the most beautiful of all U.S. coins. It's also one of the most misunderstood. Soon after this lovely coin made its first appearance in 1916, many Americans came to the conclusion that the figure portrayed on its obverse must be Mercury, the messenger of the gods in Roman mythology, because of the winged cap "he" wore. In fact, the figure is female — a classical depiction of Miss Liberty — and the coin's designer, sculptor Adolph A. Weinman, intended her wings to symbolize "liberty of thought." Although the misnomer "Mercury dime" has stuck to this coin ever since, its proper appellation is the Winged Liberty Head — or simply Winged Liberty — dime.

Just as a rose by any other name would smell as sweet, the Winged Liberty dime remains a magnificent coin no matter how inaccurately it may be described. The amazing thing about its aesthetic brilliance is that the artist achieved this despite having such a tiny "canvas" to work with. The modern U.S. dime is just 17.9 millimeters — less than three-quarters of an inch — in diameter, so this coin is truly a miniature masterpiece. The fasces, the Roman symbol of authority depicted on its reverse, later became associated with Italian dictator Benito Mussolini, but this can hardly be held against Weinman or the remarkable coin he designed.

The beauty of any coin can be seen to maximum advantage on proof examples. Unfortunately, the United States Mint was not producing annual proofs during much of the lifetime of the Winged Liberty dime, from 1916 to 1945. It did make them, though, for seven of the thirty years in which the coin was issued — from 1936 through 1942 — so these spectacular pieces do exist. The proofs from the 1930s all have mintages below 10,000 and tend to be more expensive, especially in the case of the 1936. Those from 1940 through 1942 have slightly higher mintages but are still scarce, and they can be acquired in Proof-65 for not much more than $100 apiece — about one-fifth what they were bringing in 1989. Truly, these are beautiful investments.

L O S E R   N O .   3 1

A roll of common-date Mercury dimes in average uncirculated condition

It's hard to imagine today, but not so many years ago buying modern coins by the roll was a major preoccupation of many — if not most — buyers and sellers. In the superheated market of the early 1960s, so-called collectors competed tooth and nail for the right to acquire such prizes as fifty-piece rolls of 1955-S Lincoln cents (at about $1 per coin) and forty-piece rolls of 1950-D Jefferson nickels (at up to $30 per coin). In some respects, this was not unlike a Ponzi scheme, for the only way most late-date cents and nickels could hold those values — or continue going up — was for new buyers to enter the market in increments of fifty for each available cent roll and forty for each nickel roll. Clearly, that was not about to happen.

Not all coin rolls offered for sale at that time were bad

investments, however. Sprinkled among the ads for late-date Lincoln cent and Jefferson nickel rolls were offerings of uncirculated rolls — or possibly half-rolls — of somewhat earlier coins, such as Buffalo nickels, Winged Liberty ("Mercury") dimes and Walking Liberty half dollars. And while the dates being offered were almost always common ones in those series, these coins — unlike later-date Lincolns and Jeffersons — hadn't been set aside in uncirculated condition to nearly the same extent. As a result, they're worth much more today than they were in the early 1960s.

Rolls of these coins — especially Mercury dimes from the later years of that series — are advertised occasionally today. Typically, they are priced at hundreds of dollars per roll. Chances are that this time, though, these coins are poor investments. First and foremost, the premium value of high-quality coins is so much greater today that these rolls almost certainly have been cherrypicked. You'll be lucky to find anything that's better than Mint State-60 or 61. Beyond that, buyers today favor individual coins in choice condition. The last thing they want is a roll of coins in less than top shape.

Photo courtesy of Bowers and Merena.

W I N N E R   N O .   3 2

Common-date Barber silver coins in Mint State-64 or 65, or Proof-64 or 65

Charles E. Barber was the U.S. Mint's chief sculptor-engraver for nearly four decades, from 1879 to 1917 — longer by far than any other occupant of that job. During that time, he had a hand in designing a number of new coins, including the Liberty Head nickel, the flowing-hair Stella (or $4 gold piece), the Columbian half dollar — the nation's very first commemorative coin — and several other silver and gold commemoratives. Some would say he also had a hand in sabotaging other designers' work; he has been widely criticized for reducing the relief overzealously on Augustus Saint-Gaudens' double eagle and James Earle Fraser's Buffalo nickel. Of all his coinage accomplishments, though, none is identified more closely with Charles Barber — or represents a finer legacy — than the turn-of-the-century half dollar, quarter and dime.

Throughout the first century of U.S. coinage, the half dollar, quarter and dime — joined for long stretches by the silver dollar and half dime — had been uniform in design at any given time. Barber continued this practice with his look-alike designs for the three new silver coins of 1892. Each depicts the head of Miss Liberty on the obverse, facing right, and the half dollar and quarter also share a common heraldic-eagle portrait on the reverse. Being too small for the eagle, the dime's reverse bears only the words ONE DIME within a wreath. These coins may not have been soaring works of art, but they were well-suited symbolically for the period when they were issued, from 1892 through 1916. And they wore extremely well, circulating all the way into the 1950s.

Unlike Morgan dollars, which saw only limited use, the Barber coins served Americans long and well in commerce, and relatively few were preserved in mint condition. As a result, they're elusive in high mint-state grades. You can expect to pay hundreds of dollars for even a common-date example in Mint State-64 or 65 — and more for a Proof-64 or 65, for proof mintages rarely exceeded 1,000. But these coins are legitimately scarce and the prices are justified.

L O S E R   N O .   3 2

A complete set of average uncirculated Franklin half dollars

The Franklin half dollar is a coin with a pleasing appearance whose broad, open design features two of the most admired icons from this nation's Revolutionary period: Benjamin Franklin and the Liberty Bell. It was issued for a relatively brief span — from 1948 through 1963 — before giving way to the Kennedy half dollar in the traumatic days following the assassination of President John F. Kennedy. It has only 35 date-and-mint varieties and its lowest-mintage coin, the 1953, isn't terribly scarce with a figure of nearly 2.8 million. And it has the distinction of being the last circulating U.S. coin struck entirely in silver — that is to say, the traditional U.S. coinage alloy of 90-percent silver and 10-percent copper.

Given all this, you might assume that assembling a set of Franklin half dollars in attractive mint condition would be easy and inexpensive. After all, this is a modern coin that presumably was saved in significant quantities by the roll — or even the bag — when it was new. And you would be correct — to a point. Many Franklin halves were preserved in mint condition and can be obtained today for modest premiums. But few Franklin halves existed to begin with in extremely high condition with sharp strikes and fully defined details. And those coins today bring — and deserve to bring — very high premiums, while typical BU Franklins are cheap and deservedly so.

The *Coin Dealer Newsletter* (or "Greysheet") shows a bid price, at this writing, of $260 for a set of uncirculated Franklin half dollars. This corresponds to a set in which the coins average Mint State-63. That may seem inexpensive, but it really isn't a bargain, since Franklins in that grade are generally quite common. What's more, there's a hidden danger: Often, the common dates will be nice BU coins but the key dates, such as the 1949-D and S, will be sliders. The set will look appealing as a whole, but the coins that should represent most of the value won't be worth much of a premium because they aren't really uncirculated. That's a double whammy.

Photo courtesy of Bowers and Merena.

WINNER NO. 33

Twenty-cent pieces certified as Mint State-63 or 64, or Proof-63 or 64

The twenty-cent piece may have been the most unnecessary coin in U.S. history. It certainly was one of the most unsuccessful: It was struck for circulation for only two years before being reduced to a proof-only issue. Then, after just two more years on that life-support status, it rode — or rather, limped — into the sunset. Yet, in a sense, this odd silver coin went to heaven when it died, for it has enjoyed a highly successful afterlife as a collectible.

There was no real reason to issue such a coin, at least from the perspective of the American public. But silver miners in the West were awash in precious metal at the time the coin was authorized in 1875. Nevada's Comstock Lode had done for silver mining what Sutter's Mill had done for gold mining twenty-five years earlier — and yet, with all this silver pouring into the marketplace, the Mint Act of 1873 had removed a major outlet by halting further production of silver dollars. Outraged silver miners and their friends on Capitol Hill soon began seeking new coinage uses for the metal — and one of the dividends, from the miners' point of view, was the twenty-cent piece.

Aside from the fact that it served no useful purpose not accomplished already by two dimes, the twenty-cent piece suffered from bad design work. It looked much the same as the Seated Liberty quarter — and since it was the same composition and close to the same size, people confused the two coins. The eagle on its reverse faced the other way and the edge of the coin was smooth, rather than reeded (as on the quarter) — but these were subtle differences, and in the big picture the coins were too close in appearance. In 1878, the silver interests got a new dollar coin and last rites were held for the twenty-cent piece. Its rebirth as a collectible stems not from its short life span, but rather from its very low mintages. At just over 1.1 million, the 1875-S is the "common" coin in the series. The others range from extremely scarce to downright rare. You'll pay about $600 in MS-63 and $1,000 in MS-64, and twice those amounts for the corresponding proofs. But when it comes to investment, these coins have lots of life in them.

LOSER NO. 33

Oversized replicas of U.S. coins struck privately in silver

They say that big is beautiful. "They," in this case, tend to be advertisers pushing lines of clothing for people of greater-than-usual girth. I have no quarrel with this; beauty, after all, is always in the eye of the beholder — and if special clothing will help a bigger man or woman look more beautiful to a favorite beholder, so much the better. I do have a problem, however, with advertisers who hype the bigness — and the beauty — of oversized silver "collectibles" that are based all too closely on genuine U.S. coins (and sometimes on U.S. paper money). For the strong suggestion here is that the collectibility, legitimacy and investment potential of the actual U.S. coins somehow rub off on these hefty replicas. I can assure you they do not.

Let's get one thing straight before we go any further: These replicas are *not* U.S. government issues, no matter how official they may look, or how hard the clever advertisers work to blur the line. I decided to include them on my blacklist of "coin" losers not because they are coins, but rather because many potential buyers view them as a coin-related investment, and the advertisers foster that illusion. The language in the ads seems purposely designed to mislead unwary consumers into believing these offers are being made by an arm — or at least a close affiliate — of the federal government. The company will identify itself, for example, as "the National Mint" or "the Federal Mint" — names that suggest a link with Uncle Sam. There will be the ubiquitous certificate of authenticity — a guarantee essentially that the replicas contain the advertised amount of precious metal, which isn't really at issue. Most of all, the consumer will be overwhelmed and disarmed by that big, beautiful photograph showing what he or she knows to be a genuine (though now obsolete) U.S. coin design — only in a much larger reincarnation.

The bottom line is, these replicas are nothing more than super-sized silver bars, worth only the value of the metal they contain — and yet they are priced much higher, as if they were coin collectibles. The only thing they will collect is dust; the only thing you will collect is red ink.

Photo courtesy of Bowers and Merena.

WINNER NO. 34

A Hawaiian commemorative half dollar graded Mint State-64

U.S. commemorative coinage got off to a fast start in 1892 and picked up healthy momentum during its first quarter century — but by the 1920s, it began to veer out of control and came to have a stigma attached to it. The frantic pace of new issues, the growing number and length of multi-year series, the excessively high mintages authorized for some programs, the often dubious nature of the subjects being honored, the questionable manner in which the proceeds sometimes were distributed — these and other concerns clouded U.S. commemoratives, especially when these programs shifted into overdrive during the 1930s.

Not every program stirred criticism, though. Now and then, the process worked like a charm and everyone went away with a sense of satisfaction. It can be argued that no single program accomplished this more successfully than the one that led to the issuance of the Hawaiian Sesquicentennial half dollar in 1928. Here was a perfect blend of fitting theme, appealing design, modest mintage, broad distribution, and, ultimately, a coin that has remained not only an attractive collectible but also an outstanding investment for nearly three-quarters of a century.

By 1928, Hawaii was midway between its annexation by the United States in 1898 and its admission as the 50th state in the Union in 1959. It paused on this path to Americanization to celebrate a milestone from its past: the 150th anniversary of the island chain's discovery in 1778 by British explorer James Cook. As part of this observance, Congress approved the issuance of a special half dollar — and, for once, the implementation was flawless. The coin bore handsome portraits of Captain Cook on the obverse and a native chieftain on the reverse; its mintage was held to 10,000; and despite a quick sellout, its distribution was equitable. It has been a big winner ever since. In Mint State-65, it's priced today at about $4,000. You can buy it in MS-64, just one grade lower, for half that amount. I recommend it highly.

LOSER NO. 34

Sets of 1948 and 1951 Booker T. Washington commemorative half dollars

B y the late 1940s, commemorative coinage had fallen into disfavor with the U.S. government — and even with many collectors. Production of commemoratives had been on hold during World War II, but rather than being lifted after the end of the war, the suspension soon gave way to a virtual ban. Two new programs did win approval from Congress right after the war, and one of these — the Booker T. Washington Memorial half dollar — spawned a related coin honoring both Washington and a second black leader, George Washington Carver. But after the conclusion of the Washington-Carver program in 1954, no new U.S. commemoratives would appear for twenty-eight years. The abuses surrounding such coins had left a sour taste in many people's mouths and built up a resistance to further issues.

The first postwar commemorative, the Iowa half dollar of

1946, was a one-year issue marking a statehood centennial —
a theme that clearly merited such a coin. But the two subsequent coins, while laudable for honoring the achievements of
black Americans, repeated some of the worst abuses linked to
the many "commems" of the 1930s. The authorized mintage
of 5 million Booker T. Washington halves (later shared with
the Washington-Carver coin) was far too high. The programs
were permitted to linger far too long, extending all the way
from 1946 through 1954, with both types being produced in
1951. And serious questions arose as to whether the proceeds
were benefiting worthy programs for blacks or simply lining
the pockets of opportunistic sponsors.

Many Booker T. Washington halves went unsold and
eventually were melted. More than 1.7 million survived,
though — an enormously high mintage by the standards of
"traditional" U.S. commemoratives. Further depressing their
value, many were mishandled at the time of original sale.
Typically, these coins are sold even now in date-mint sets of
P-D-S (Philadelphia, Denver and San Francisco) issues. The
1948 and 1951 sets are the No. 1 losers among pre-1955 U.S.
commemoratives, according to noted expert Anthony
Swiatek. Their prices range from $110 to $135 in Mint
State-63 or 64, but they're ultra-common and all too often
scuffed and unappealing.

Photo courtesy of Bowers and Merena.

W I N N E R   N O .   3 5

Nickel three-cent pieces certified as Mint State-66 or 67

We've all heard it said that you shouldn't judge a book by its cover. For much the same reason, you shouldn't judge a coin by its mintage. Many coins that were made in meaningful quantities — even by the millions — are scarce or even rare in very high levels of preservation. Through wide circulation, mishandling and other attrition, the mountain that existed at the time the coins were minted has shrunk to just a molehill in very high mint condition. The coins may be abundant in circulated grades and in lower mint-state levels, and yet be downright rare in grades above Mint State-65 — the so-called "super-grade" range.

Nickel three-cent pieces illustrate this point. These curious relics of the Reconstruction period after the Civil War were struck in significant numbers at the outset: Between their introduction in 1865 and 1870, more than 25 million pieces were produced. But those coins saw extensive use, for they were sorely needed at a time when subsidiary silver coins — including the dime and half dime — hadn't yet begun to circulate widely again after being hoarded during the war. Only a relative handful of nickel three-cent pieces from that early period ended up being preserved in pristine

Photo courtesy of Bowers and Merena.

condition. Then, beginning in 1871, mintages dropped sharply as the new Shield nickel proved to be more popular with the public. Only proofs were issued in 1877 and 1878 — and after one last burst of more than 1 million pieces in 1881, minuscule numbers of business strikes were issued through the end of the series in 1889.

Elsewhere in this book, I recommend nickel three-cent pieces in Proof-66 as one of my winners. Those are certainly rare and desirable, but these coins are even rarer in Mint State-66 and higher grades. The mintage figures won't tell you that, for proofs exceeded 5,000 in only one year and fell below 1,000 in ten other years. But many of those proofs were saved in top condition, and few of the business strikes were.

L O S E R   N O .   3 5

The 1887/6 P-mint Morgan dollar graded Mint State-64 and higher

Overdates are among the most dramatic — and sometimes the most valuable — of mint-error U.S. coins. They were relatively common during the early years of the U.S. Mint, when budget constraints were severe, equipment was unsophisticated and dies were often reused from one year to the next in an effort to hold down costs. They occurred far less frequently after the conversion to steam-powered coinage in the mid–1830s, for the technological upgrade greatly enhanced the quality of the coins and quality control at the Mint. And they've all but disappeared in the twentieth century — to the point that when they do appear, they bring exceptional premiums.

Typically, overdates have resulted when a die remained unused — or only lightly used — at the end of a calendar year and Mint technicians engraved a new last number over the old one so the die could continue to be used in the new year. On occasion, this process involved the last two numbers in the date — or even the last three, as when a die for 1798 cents was retooled for use in 1800. Because they occurred so frequently and were struck in such meaningful numbers, early U.S. overdates often command little or no more than regular coins from the same years. But modern U.S. overdates are quite a different story: The 1918/17-D Buffalo nickel, 1918/17-S Standing Liberty quarter and 1942/41 Mercury dime all bring thousands of dollars in mint condition.

The 1887/6 Morgan dollar is far from common. But it also doesn't seem to be nearly as rare as the two 1918 overdates. And though it is part of a highly collected series, it never has attracted a fervent following. Undoubtedly this stems, in large measure, from the fact that the "6" isn't readily visible underneath the "7" in the date. It's so well concealed, in fact, that the overdate wasn't discovered until 1971. There are 1887/6 overdate dollars from both Philadelphia and New Orleans, with the O-mint coin being scarcer and more expensive. At $900 in MS-64 and $3,000 in MS-65, the P-mint overdate appears to be overpriced, since hundreds of examples have been certified in those grades. The supply exceeds the demand, and I would avoid this coin.

Photo courtesy of Ed Reiter

WINNER NO. 36

Lower-mintage American Eagle bullion coins, under certain circumstances

Not every "winner" comes without strings. Some are good values only to a point, or only under certain circumstances; and the number of strings attached may vary considerably from one item to another. I'm attaching several very important strings in recommending the purchase of American Eagle gold, silver and platinum bullion coins.

American Eagles made their first appearance in 1986, when the U.S. Mint introduced the one-ounce silver Eagle plus gold Eagles in four different versions: the basic one-ounce size and subsidiary sizes of 1/2, 1/4 and 1/10 of an ounce. The platinum Eagle was added to the roster in 1997, and comes in the same four versions as its gold counterpart. As bullion coins, all of the business-strike American Eagles vary in price according to the value of the metal they contain: The price at any given time reflects their bullion value plus a small surcharge to cover the costs of production, distribution and marketing. (This does not pertain to the proof American Eagles, which are listed as a "loser" elsewhere in this book.)

In theory, bullion coins are not numismatic in nature and bring no added premium as collectibles. In practice, some collectors do place added value on certain bullion coins when their mintages fall significantly below the normal production levels for their series. This premium may be modest, but it could have the potential to rise in years to come if a particular series continues to be produced and grows in popularity, thus expanding the circle of potential buyers for low-mintage dates. This brings me to the strings. I recommend these coins only if you pay no bonus premium to begin with (over the regular surcharge), and only if you buy them at a time when the price of bullion is not inflated. Half-ounce and quarter-ounce gold and platinum Eagles are especially good possibilities, since their mintages tend to be much lower than the one-ounce and tenth-ounce pieces. Michael R. Fuljenz of Universal Coins in Beaumont, Texas, says these coins offer what he calls a "double play" over ordinary bullion coins.

L O S E R   N O .   3 6

An uncirculated roll of 1955 Franklin half dollars

Throughout U.S. history, production of coins has tended to reflect the condition of the national economy. When peace and prosperity reigned supreme, mintages often were high, for more coins were needed to keep the wheels of commerce turning smoothly. When times were bad, the flow of coins sometimes slowed to a trickle, since people were spending less money. That's what happened during the Great Depression, for example. The cent was the only U.S. coin minted every year from 1930 through 1934; and from 1931 through 1933, fewer Lincoln cents were made than in any similar period in the history of this venerable coin.

In 1954, midway through Dwight D. Eisenhower's first term in the White House, the nation was gripped by a serious recession, the worst economic slump since the Depression. The malaise carried over into 1955, sharply reducing demand for new coinage that year. As a result, mintages of 1955 coins were far lower than usual right across the board. The 1955-S Lincoln cent, the 1955 Jefferson nickel, the 1955-P, D and S Roosevelt dimes and the 1955-D Washington quarter all are among the lowest-mintage coins struck in these series since the end of World War II.

The Franklin half dollar also felt the impact of the cutback. No halves were struck in 1955 at Denver and San Francisco, the two branch mints then in operation, and the main mint in Philadelphia turned out fewer than 2.9 million, the second-lowest mintage in the series (the 1953 being lower by a total of less than 80,000). This would seem to make the '55 half dollar a desirable collectible. It does bring a premium, partly because of its mintage and partly because it is silver: An uncirculated roll is selling at this writing for $115, a bit under $6 per coin. But even at that modest price, it's no great bargain. Speculators saved this coin by the bagful at the time it was issued. And chances are any roll you buy today will contain only marginal mint-state coins; any real gems that might have been there in 1955 will be long gone.

The 1861-O Liberty Head double eagle graded AU-50

With the outbreak of the Civil War on April 12, 1861, three of the four branch U.S. mints then in operation were behind Confederate lines. Only the main mint in Philadelphia and the branch in San Francisco remained in Union hands. The War Between the States was the death knell for the mints in Charlotte, North Carolina, and Dahlonega, Georgia, but the third Southern mint, at New Orleans, resumed its role as a federal institution in the late 1870s, first as an assay office in 1876 and then as a mint in 1879. It continued producing coins until 1909.

Limited numbers of U.S. coins were struck at New Orleans in 1861, before and after the mint fell into Confederate hands. It actually functioned as a federal agency only for a month that year: The state of Louisiana took charge of all operations on January 31, 1861, and the Confederate States of America then assumed control on March 31. Old records show the Confederate forces found more than $200,000 worth of bullion in the vaults and struck this into coinage, using U.S. dies, before closing the mint on May 31 because it had no further metal to coin.

Half dollars and double eagles ($20 gold pieces) were the only coins produced in New Orleans in that fateful first year of the war. The half dollar mintage was relatively high, totaling more than 2.5 million — and even though most of these were struck under state or Confederate auspices, all were made with U.S. dies, so there's no way of telling them apart. (It's believed that four half dollars bearing a Confederate reverse also were minted in 1861 in New Orleans.) By contrast, the O-mint produced just 17,741 double eagles —

presumably because it ran out of bullion at that point. These are virtually unknown in mint condition and the few known examples bring exceptional premiums, starting at $18,000 in Mint State-60. Even then, you're apt to find wear on the high points. Nice examples graded About Uncirculated-50 can be had for $6,500 or so, and I recommend these. They're rare coins from a pivotal year in U.S. and U.S. Mint history.

Photo courtesy of Bowers and Merena.

LOSER NO. 37

Saint-Gaudens double eagles graded Mint State-66 and 67

It probably seems incongruous — even absurd — to apply the term "loser" to the beautiful Saint-Gaudens double eagle. This magnificent coin has long been acclaimed by collectors and critics alike as the finest work of numismatic art ever to emerge from the U.S. Mint. The label must seem doubly inappropriate when it is assigned to "Saints" in very high levels of preservation. Those, after all, display the coin's beauty at its dazzling best, with a minimum of flaws and a maximum of mint luster and sharp detail.

The problem lies not with the coin, but rather with its price. Precisely because it *is* so beautiful and desirable, this $20 gold piece has been hyped extensively as an investment vehicle for well-heeled buyers outside the hobby. Lacking in-depth knowledge about rare coins and a sense of involve-ment with the hobby, these buyers have proven to be extremely fickle, abandoning their coin investments at the first sign of market weakness. Demand for high-grade Saints can therefore be quite unpredictable. At the same time, there has been a dramatic increase in the available supply as more and more coins have been certified by the third-party grading services. As of January 1997, the Professional Coin Grading Service and the Numismatic Guaranty Corporation of America had certified a combined total of 4,059 Saints as MS-66 and 99 as MS-67. By January 1998, these figures had risen to 14,018 and 236, respectively — and there could be many more where those came from.

At this writing, Saints are priced at $2,200 in MS-66 and $9,000 in MS-67. Those are hefty premiums for coins that are so susceptible to sharp declines in demand and major increases in supply. The coins are truly spectacular, but right now the prices are wrong. Beautiful coins aren't necessarily beautiful investments as well.

Photo courtesy of Bowers and Merena.

WINNER NO. 38

The 1885-CC Morgan dollar graded Mint State-65

In recent years, the term "condition rarity" has become an important part of the coin market's lexicon. This phrase describes a coin that may be rather common — with a modest price to match — in lower grade levels, but is scarce or flat-out rare and brings a first-rate premium in pristine mint condition. The Morgan dollar series includes a number of coins that fit this description. Consider, for example, the 1886-O. This coin can be purchased for $10 or less in Very Fine — a mid-level circulated grade — but its price soars into the thousands in Mint State-63, into the tens of thousands in Mint State-65 and into the hundreds of thousands in Mint State-66.

Accurate grading is crucial when just a small difference in grade can translate into a difference of many thousands of dollars in market value. Likewise, it is essential to preserve such a coin with extraordinary care and protect it from the slightest imperfection. Even then, there is a risk that the price of a mint-state specimen could be affected adversely — and possibly plunge precipitously — if hitherto unknown supplies of the coin turn up in top condition. After all, the New Orleans Mint made 10.7 million dollars in 1886.

No such worries exist with a silver dollar struck just one year earlier at the Carson City Mint. The 1885-CC Morgan dollar is rare in every condition because the Nevada mint produced just 228,000 cartwheels that year, the fourth-lowest mintage in the Morgan series. A circulated piece will cost you much more than the corresponding 1886-O; even in the lowly grade of Very Good, for instance, the '85-CC dollar sells for nearly $150. But there are no huge increments as you go up the grading scale. On the contrary, the jumps are quite small until you reach the high mint-state range. This rare-date coin can be obtained for less than $500 in MS-65 and less than $1,000 in MS-66. True, this reflects the fact that much of the mintage survives in uncirculated condition, having been stored for decades in U.S. Treasury vaults. But given the low mintage, the current market values have a bedrock base of rarity. And you can go to bed not having to worry that your rare, beautiful coin — struck at a colorful mint spawned by the historic Comstock Lode — will have lost much of its value overnight.

L O S E R   N O .   3 8

Legal-tender coins produced by private mints such as The Franklin Mint

There is a long tradition in the United States of private companies striking fine-art medals. The earliest presidential inaugural badges and medals, for example, were produced by such firms as Whitehead and Hoag of Newark, N.J., and the Joseph K. Davison Company of Philadelphia. Later, Medallic Art Company of New York City played a key role in designing and producing inaugural medals — as well as other medals, such as the twice-yearly Society of Medalists issues.

None of this adequately prepared the numismatic community for the whirlwind arrival of a new kind of private minter in the mid-1960s. Founded in 1965 as General Numismatics Corporation, the company soon transformed itself into a marketing giant known as The Franklin Mint. Instead of producing and selling art medals one at a time, this new "mint" launched whole series of glitzy silver medals built around such themes as "The History of the United States" and "The Genius of Michelangelo." A typical series consisted of perhaps sixty one-ounce silver proof medals that would be shipped one a month until the collection was completed. Orders would be "limited" — but only to the number submitted by a given deadline (only one subscription per customer, please).

The Franklin Mint spawned numerous imitators, and for a time the marketplace was deluged not only with private medals but also with such related items as ingots, bars, plates and even spoons. Eventually, the craze subsided and the companies either diversified or withered on the vine. Some, including The Franklin Mint, used their production capacity to strike increasing numbers of legal-tender coins for foreign governments. But the customers tended to be small nations seeking big revenue from selling "collectible" coins at inflated prices. Some of these coins are gold or platinum; others come in sets or whole series. Either way, they can cost many hundreds of dollars. They're not worth it, and you should avoid them like the plague they are.

Photo courtesy of Bowers and Merena.

WINNER NO. 39

Type II and III Liberty Head double eagles graded Mint State-60 through 63

The Saint-Gaudens double eagle is the superstar of U.S. gold coinage, and the elegant, full-length Liberty depicted on its obverse is the glamorous leading lady who always gets rave reviews from all the critics. The Liberty Head that adorns all previous double eagles seems matronly and sedate — perhaps a character actress — by comparison. Looks can be deceiving, though, for while those earlier coins are clearly not as glitzy and lack the marquee value of the aptly nicknamed "Saints," they're often more solid performers at the box office for their backers — the collectors and investors who rely on them as a source of financial gain. Put another way, Liberty Head double eagles — particularly the later ones — are generally scarcer and more valuable than the glamour-puss coins that succeeded them.

The double eagle, or $20 gold piece, came into being in 1849 as a direct result of the California Gold Rush. Needing new ways to utilize all the gold that was pouring into the marketplace, Congress authorized two new gold coins — this nearly one-ounce heavyweight and the tiny gold dollar — to help soak up the excess supply. The basic design of the Liberty double eagle remained much the same throughout its more than fifty-year run, but collectors recognize three distinct types. The original version gave way to Type II in 1866, when the motto IN GOD WE TRUST was added to the reverse. Then, in 1877, Type III came about when the statement of value was changed from the shorthand TWENTY D. to TWENTY DOLLARS.

Michael R. Fuljenz of Universal Coin and Bullion in Beaumont, Texas, reports that Type II and III examples of this coin are "much rarer" than Saints in mint condition — presumably because they weren't set aside to nearly the same extent when they were new. Original bags of Saints turn up much more frequently, and in much larger quantities, than bags of mint-state Liberties, Fuljenz says. And when gold bullion goes up in value, late-date "Libs" tend to rise the fastest.

LOSER NO. 39

Fractional gold pieces graded Mint State-63 through 65

Good things come in small packages, or so we are told. In practice, of course, this is true only part of the time. Even when good things do come in small packages, they may be good only to a point, or only under certain circumstances. If that point is exceeded, or those circumstances cease to exist, the contents of those "packages" may not be so good after all. Consider the case of the fractional gold coins minted in California during and after the famous Gold Rush.

California was awash in gold dust and nuggets in the early 1850s as prospectors worked their claims and brought their ore to market. What it lacked most conspicuously was a standard and convenient medium of exchange — in short, small coinage — since gold in raw form left much to be desired in this regard. To fill this pressing need, private minters began producing small gold coin substitutes in 1852, assigning denominations of dollar, half dollar and quarter dollar. These supplemented the higher-value gold pieces, in denominations of $5 through $50, which also were being privately struck at that time. The small-denomination gold pieces assumed a lesser role following the opening of the San Francisco Mint in 1854, which soon provided the region with official U.S. coinage of comparable face value. They remained popular, though, as souvenirs and continued to be minted until 1882.

Thousands of these small gold pieces survive today, in hundreds of different varieties. Many are quite rare, and all command at least modest premiums. Typically, they are worth about $500 each in mid-range mint condition — the range represented by MS-63 through 65. Pricing them is difficult, however, because they are so rare and esoteric. And, for this reason, unscrupulous telemarketers love to sell them, frequently charging five, ten or twenty times their actual market value. Thus, while these small "packages" are surely rare and valuable — in other words, good — they are overpriced so often that it would be advisable to avoid them as if they were really *bad*.

An 1877-S Liberty Head double eagle graded Mint State-62

At first glance, the 1877-S Liberty Head double eagle (or $20 gold piece) seems to be a coin of no particular interest, with a relatively high mintage by the standards of its series and denomination. Indeed, at 1,735,000, it has the second-highest mintage of any "Lib $20" struck between 1862 and 1897 — just 4,000 pieces behind the pacesetter, the 1878-S. On closer inspection, however, this turns out to be a rare coin in pristine mint condition — in fact, in any grade above the modest level of Mint State-62.

There are various reasons why a coin produced in large numbers may be surprisingly scarce in high grades. One of the most common explanations is that the coin had generally poor quality to begin with, so few, if any, examples existed in flawless condition even on the day they left the mint. That's a major reason so many of our modern copper-nickel "clad" coins are elusive in the upper-end mint-state grades. Mishandling is another contributing factor, and this appears to have been a serious problem with Liberty Head double eagles. The late Walter Breen, perhaps the most renowned of all numismatic researchers, reported in his *Complete Encyclopedia of U.S. and Colonial Coins* that many of these large gold coins "occur without discernible wear but with some hair and feather details obscured by bag marks." He went on to say that these coins usually are regarded, and priced, as AU, rather than uncirculated.

Whatever the reason, experience has shown that the 1877-S double eagle is rare in even mid-level mint-state grades, and this is reflected in its price: It brings more than $10,000 in MS-63. By contrast, it is readily available in grades below that level, selling for a much more affordable $1,500 in

MS-62, just a single grade down the ladder on the 1-to-70 scale. As you might expect, that makes it quite easy to sell this coin when it is certified as MS-62. The chances of getting it regraded as MS-63 are remote, since the grading services are keenly aware of the price gap and reluctant to create instant wealth. But buyers are comfortable with the lower price.

LOSER NO. 40

The 1842-C small-date half eagle graded EF-45

The branch U.S. mints at Charlotte, North Carolina, and Dahlonega, Georgia, came into being in the late 1830s because of the discovery of gold in the southern Appalachian Mountains. Transporting the ore to the Philadelphia Mint was a major inconvenience for the miners, and they had been seeking the establishment of such mints since the gold rush began in the 1820s. When Congress was slow to respond, private minters began accepting deposits instead — and that spurred the federal government into action.

The Charlotte and Dahlonega mints began producing coins in 1838 — and from then until 1861, when the Civil War broke out and they were forced to close, their output consisted entirely of gold coins, usually of relatively inferior quality and very low mintage levels. Today, many of these coins, with their odd and distinctive "C" or "D" mint marks, command substantial premiums over their higher-mintage counterparts from Philadelphia, New Orleans and San Francisco. They're particularly scarce and valuable in mint condition because of the chronic technical deficiencies that plagued them throughout the existence of these small Southern mints.

Although these coins are legitimately scarce — and even

downright rare — in many instances, this is not always the case. And sometimes, through shrewd promotion or simple miscalculation by buyers and sellers, the rarity of certain C- and D-mint gold coins is perceived to be greater than it is, resulting in inflated price levels. A case in point is the 1842 small-date half eagle (or $5 gold piece) from the Charlotte Mint. As this is written in May 1998, this coin is valued at $42,500 in Extremely Fine-45 by the leading price guides — triple what it was bringing just a year ago. Lee Minshull, a dealer who handles many rare-date gold coins, says he knows of one collector who has amassed twenty-five examples in high circulated grades. Dealers have been promoting this coin, he says, because it is available in quantity in such grades. He places its true value at closer to $20,000. The moral: Beware of promotions, even when a coin may seem rare and obscure.

The 1838 Coronet eagle graded Extremely Fine

The eagle, or $10 gold piece, had the highest face value of any coin in Uncle Sam's original coinage lineup — the one that was authorized by Congress in the Mint Act of 1792. It would remain the highest-denomination U.S. coin for more than half a century before being supplanted in 1849 by the double eagle. For most of that time, however, it would not be in the lineup as an active "player": It was not produced at all for more than three decades, from 1805 through 1837.

When the Mint did resume production of the eagle in 1838, it used a new design prepared by engraver Christian Gobrecht, an artist better known for his work on the silver coinage of that period, especially the so-called "Gobrecht dollar." For the obverse, he fashioned a left-facing portrait of Liberty with a coronet in her hair — a portrait closely resembling the one he designed for the cent the following year. For the reverse, he modified the heraldic eagle created for the earlier Capped Bust coinage by another Mint engraver, John Reich. Partway through production in 1839, the size of the inscriptions was reduced. As a result, collectors now recognize — and pursue — both "large letters" and "small letters" varieties, with the earlier version being a two-year type coin.

The 1838 eagle is highly desirable — and extremely collectible — for several reasons. It's the first-year issue in a series that extended for seven decades before giving way to Augustus Saint-Gaudens' Indian Head eagle in 1907. Its mintage is minuscule: just 7,200 pieces. And it's one of just two dates with large letters. This coin is almost unobtainable

Photo courtesy of Bowers and Merena.

in choice mint condition and brings $20,000 or more even in the barely uncirculated grade of Mint State-60. Yet as of this writing, it's priced at just $2,900 in Extremely Fine. Lee Minshull, a dealer who handles many early U.S. gold coins, considers this a real bargain: It is, he says, at least 30 percent below what the coin is really worth. Looking at the figures, I agree with him.

LOSER NO. 41

Coins from buried treasure, shipwrecks and hoards

Buried treasure has always held great allure for men of adventure and action. The thought of discovering old oaken chests full of hidden pirate booty — or sunken Spanish galleons at the bottom of the sea with cargos of glittering gold — can fire the imagination like few other visions known to man. Ironically, however, the existence of such treasure in centuries-old graves can jeopardize the value of wealth already secured in safes and under mattresses. Likewise, coins held in hoards for many years can depress market values for similar coins already in collections.

Gold is impervious, or at least highly resistant, to damage from natural forces such as water coursing through a sunken ship. As a consequence, golden treasure recovered from salvaged ships often will betray little evidence of the elements to which it has been subjected. Gold coins, in particular, have emerged from such vessels in remarkably high levels of preservation. And, in recent years, as technology has improved and the heightened price of gold has justified greater outlays by investors, salvagers have grown more and more aggressive in exploring shipwreck sites — and more and more successful in finding and recovering long-lost treasure.

The 1854-S double eagle, the very first $20 gold piece struck at the fledgling San Francisco Mint, has turned up in meaningful quantities in the bowels of several salvaged nineteenth century ships, including the *SS Yankee Blade* and the *SS Central America*. Discoveries such as these can destabilize — and reduce — the value of scarce-date gold coins as collectibles. This has happened already with the 1854-S double eagle, a better-date coin worth thousands of dollars in mint condition. And it can happen again as new treasure is salvaged and hits the market. Similarly, the market is now absorbing some 15,000 high-grade examples of the 1908 no-motto Saint-Gaudens double eagle that came from the so-called Wells-Fargo Hoard. Until this process of absorption is complete, this overhang is bound to hold prices down.

Photo courtesy of Bowers and Merena.

WINNER NO. 42

The 1875 Liberty Head eagle graded About Uncirculated-50

When is a "rare coin" really, truly rare? The answer isn't always as obvious as you might think. The 1877 Indian cent, for example, certainly is perceived as being rare and would hold a high place on most collectors' wish lists — yet it has a mintage of 852,500. There are only two half cents with mintages higher than that, yet half cents as a group are looked upon by most as scarce, rather than rare. Likewise, the 1916-D Mercury dime is viewed by just about everyone as a rare coin, but its mintage of 264,000 is higher than that of the 1869 Seated Liberty dime (256,000), which is considered a fairly common coin within its series.

In both of these examples, rarity is relative. Indian cents

are collected far more widely than half cents, so a coin can be deemed a rarity even with a mintage that would be quite high in a different series. Similarly, there are many more collectors pursuing sets of Mercury dimes than sets of Seated dimes, so the standards are much different. Intensify the demand in the law of supply and demand and you increase the value of any given coin — and value, in turn, reinforces the perception of rarity.

There are some cases, of course, where rarity is absolute — where mintages are so minuscule that everyone agrees the coins on a given list are flat-out rare. The 1875 Liberty Head eagle is such a coin. Only 100 business strikes and 20 proofs were made that year at the Philadelphia Mint, making this the lowest-mintage $10 gold piece in U.S. history. As if that didn't make it rare enough, many examples are thought to have been melted soon after being struck. Production of gold coins was at low ebb in the mid-1870s, largely because of reduced demand from banks, which were balking at redeeming paper money — including federal notes — with gold and silver coins. The 1875 eagle is all but unknown in mint condition, making AU-50 the highest collectible grade. It's priced at $120,000 even then — but other eagles from the same period with mintages in the thousands don't bring a whole lot less, so in reality this is a wonderful buy.

Photo courtesy of Bowers and Merena.

LOSER NO. 42

The 1914 Indian Head quarter eagle graded Mint State-62

Price guides are excellent tools for people who buy and sell coins. Few people — even experts — can memorize the value of every single coin, in every single grade, with unfailing accuracy, so price guides play a vital role in filling in buyers' and sellers' mental blanks. But even the finest price guides aren't perfect, and no price guide — however venerable and respected it may be — should ever be regarded as infallible.

In a fluid marketplace such as the one for coins, prices can change quickly and dramatically — so many of the prices in popular guidebooks, and even in weekly periodicals, are bound to be at variance with actual market values at any given time. I recognize this in preparing my own annual price guide, *The Insider's Guide to U.S. Coin Values*, a paperback published by Dell. I strive to make each price as accurate as possible on the date it is submitted to the publisher, taking into account any major trends I perceive, either upward or downward. But I realize that this book — and other listings like it — are, after all, simply guides, as their names suggest.

Outright mistakes are another matter. Now and then, a

price guide — or several different price guides — will list a coin's value far higher or lower than what that coin is bringing in the marketplace. Occasionally, such an error persists in future listings, rather like a lie that assumes the appearance of truth through repeated restatements. A coin such as this has fallen through the cracks, so to speak. An excellent example is the 1914 Indian Head quarter eagle certified in the grade of Mint State-62. This coin is wrongly perceived to be scarcer and more valuable than it really is. Perhaps this is because at 240,117, it has the lowest mintage of any Philadelphia issue in its series and the second-lowest overall, behind the genuinely scarce 1911-D (at 55,680). But it is only marginally scarcer than the so-called common coins in the series. And at $1,400, its price in some listings is double or more what it sells for among knowledgeable dealers and collectors. Pay that kind of money and you'll see your potential profit fall between the cracks as well — perhaps permanently.

Photo courtesy of Bowers and Merena.

WINNER NO. 43

The Sesquicentennial half dollar and quarter eagle graded Mint State-64

Over the years, a number of the commemorative coins authorized by Congress and struck by the U.S. Mint have paid tribute to people, places and events of dubious significance, at least when judged by the yardstick of national relevance. Why, critics ask, should there be federal coinage for the centennial of Fort Vancouver, Washington, the sesquicentennial of Hudson, New York, or the bicentennial of Norfolk, Virginia? All of these were basically local anniversaries of little or no interest to people living elsewhere in the nation, yet all indeed were recognized on national coinage of the realm — invariably because they had powerful advocates pushing the right buttons in Washington, D.C.

No similar objection could possibly be raised to the two special coins struck in 1926 to mark the sesquicentennial of American independence — the 150th anniversary of the fateful Fourth of July when a group of this nation's Founding Fathers gathered in Philadelphia to sign the Declaration of Independence. That, after all, was the very cornerstone of American democracy, and no other event compares with it even remotely in terms of its significance for the nation as a whole and for each and every American individually.

Considering the importance of the occasion, the coinage commemoration was very modest: Congress authorized 1 million examples of a special half dollar and 200,000 examples of a quarter eagle, or $2.50 gold piece, for sale at small premiums ($1 apiece for the half dollar, $4 each for the quarter eagle) at the Sesquicentennial Exposition in Philadelphia. Surprisingly, both coins fell far short of even those unambitious levels. Nearly 860,000 half dollars and more than 154,000 quarter eagles went unsold and were melted, leaving net mintages of 141,120 and 46,019, respectively. Both coins are notorious for weakness of strike, and both are highly elusive and extremely expensive in grades of Mint State-65 and above. The dollar jumps from $290 in MS-64 to $4,250 in MS-65, the quarter eagle from $580 to $2,550. They're just as historic in MS-64 and far more affordable — and you really don't lose all that much in aesthetic appeal.

LOSER NO. 43

The 1936 Cleveland commemorative half dollar graded Mint State-65

Cleveland is a city with much to offer. In recent years, for instance, it has become the home of the Rock-and-Roll Hall of Fame and a beautiful new stadium, Jacobs Field — and the stadium, in turn, has brought even brighter luster to the city and its people through the on-the-field success of baseball's Cleveland Indians, who play their home games there. Despite these upbeat developments, though, Cleveland continues to suffer lingering image problems because of bad publicity in the past.

Perhaps those image problems have rubbed off on the

Cleveland half dollar, the special 50-cent piece struck by the U.S. Mint in 1936 to commemorate the centennial of the city on Lake Erie's southern shore. The centennial gave rise to a celebration called the Great Lakes Exposition, which took place in Cleveland in 1936, and the coin was sold to visitors for $1.50 each to raise needed revenue to help finance that event. It's worth a good deal more than that today, but not nearly as much as some of the other commemorative coins from the same period. And, like the city it honors, it doesn't always get a lot of respect.

Congress authorized a minimum of 25,000 Cleveland half dollars and a maximum of 50,000. The Mint struck 25,000 initially — then, when those sold out, it produced the entire remaining authorization. An overhang was left when the exposition closed, but the sponsors chose not to return any unsold coins for melting, diverging in that regard from a practice that was followed with numerous other commemoratives. As a result, supplies of this coin have always been more than adequate to satisfy collector demand and prices have been modest: Even in Mint State-65, it retails as of this writing for only about $150. All of this makes the coin accessible and affordable. But since there is strong supply and limited demand, it also makes for a coin with little investment potential. In short, this is one instance where lack of respect appears to be fully justified.

Photo courtesy of Bowers and Merena.

WINNER NO. 44

An 1807 Capped Bust quarter eagle graded Extremely Fine-45

Two dollars and fifty cents won't go very far today. It's hardly enough to rent a video, much less cover the price of admission to see a first-run movie in a theater. It may be enough for a Kid's Meal at McDonald's, but it won't buy mom or dad a Big Mac. This now-puny sum was far from inconsequential, though, in America's formative years. At the start of the 19th century, $2.50 would have bought a bushel of salt — a substance essential to keep meat from spoiling in that far-off era without refrigeration. For many working people, in fact, it represented a full week's wages at the time.

It's little wonder, then, that the quarter eagle — or $2.50 gold piece — was struck in such small numbers in the period when U.S. coinage, like the nation itself, was very young. From 1796, when the coin made its first appearance, through 1807, when the initial design type — the Capped Bust Facing Right — ran its course, the quarter eagle was issued in eight different years, yet the total combined mintage for that entire period was less than 20,000. That kind of figure is looked upon as rare when it constitutes the mintage for a year, much less a series.

Photo courtesy of Bowers and Merena.

More than one-third of the Capped Bust Facing Right quarter eagles were struck in 1807, the last year before the design was changed. In fact, that year's mintage of 6,812 was more than twice the combined output of the second- and third-place years, 1804 and 1802, respectively. It's a rare coin nonetheless. And if anything, its greater availability has enhanced its popularity as a type coin, since some of the other dates are prohibitively rare, with price tags to match. Even the 1807 is all but unobtainable in uncirculated condition; it costs $15,000 in the lowest mint-state grade, MS-60. But it's far more available — and affordable — in EF-45, a grade in which it's now priced at $5,500. And a true EF specimen retains a substantial amount of mint luster. Given the rarity of any coin from this series, that's not much to pay for a piece that's bright, appealing and close to new.

LOSER NO. 44

Type II gold dollars graded Mint State-63 to 65

The tiny gold dollar is one of the smallest coins ever issued by Uncle Sam, outweighing only the wafer-thin silver three-cent piece. To put it in perspective, it weighs 26 percent less than the current Roosevelt dime. It can have big value, however, as a collectible, since its mintage figures tended to be every bit as small as the coin itself. In many cases, very large premiums are justified. But, in other instances, the price tags attached to gold dollars are bigger than they should be, given the actual rarity of the coins.

The gold dollar came into being in 1849 as a direct result of the California Gold Rush. It was one of two new coins authorized that year to help soak up the enormous new supplies of the precious yellow metal that were pouring into commerce from the West Coast. Its companion, the double eagle (or $20 gold piece), was a far more impressive store of value, containing very nearly an ounce of gold. But the dollar was envisioned as a coin that would be useful to ordinary Americans as a handier alternative to the bulky silver dollar. In practice, it would prove to be inconveniently small, just as the silver dollar was inconveniently large.

Gold dollars were produced from 1849 trough 1889. They saw limited use, however, and eventually were scrapped after years of minuscule mintages. Collectors divide the series into three types: the Liberty Head version, from 1849 to 1854; the Indian Head with a small head, from 1854 to 1856; and the Indian Head with a large head, from 1856 to 1889. Type II gold dollars include six different date-and-mint combinations whose mintages vary widely — from a mere 1,811 for the 1855-C to a comfortable 783,943 for the 1854. These are certainly scarce coins, especially in mint condition. But their relatively large certified populations don't justify the prices currently being charged for them as type coins: $12,750 in Mint State-63, $20,000 in MS-64 and $55,000 in MS-65. Mark Yaffe of the National Gold Exchange, a major gold-coin dealership in Tampa, Florida, lists these as the No. 1 loser in today's coin market.

About the author

SCOTT A. TRAVERS ranks as one of the most powerful and influential coin dealers in the world. His name is familiar to readers everywhere as the author of four best selling books on coins: *The Coin Collector's Survival Manual, How to Make Money in Coins Right Now, Travers' Rare Coin Investment Strategy* and *The Investor's Guide to Coin Trading.* All four have won book-of-the-year awards from the Numismatic Literary Guild. His introductory guide to coin collecting, *One-Minute Coin Expert,* has been called "the most important book of its kind ever written" by *COINage* magazine. And Mr. Travers is the author of one of the nation's most popular annual price guides: *The Insider's Guide to U.S. Coin Values.* He is a contributing editor to *COINage* magazine and a regular contributor to other numismatic periodicals. His opinions as an expert are often sought by publications such as *Barron's, Business Week* and *The Wall Street Journal,* and he has served as a coin valuation consultant to the Federal Trade Commission. A frequent guest on radio and television programs, Scott Travers has won awards and gained an impressive reputation not only as a coin expert but also as a forceful consumer advocate for the coin-buying public. He has coordinated the liquidation of numerous important coin collections. He is president of Scott Travers Rare Coin Galleries, Inc., in New York City.